The Fortune-Teller

Frontispiece: Victor Séjour, from *Diogène,* Mar. 8, 1857.
Cliché Bibliothèque nationale de France, Paris.

The Fortune-Teller

VICTOR SÉJOUR

Translated from the French by
Norman R. Shapiro

Introduction by M. Lynn Weiss

second
line
press

New Orleans, LA

Joseph S. Phillips and Susan J. Wood, Ph.D., Publishers
www.secondlinepress.com

Cover design: Kerrie Kemperman

ISBN-13: 978-0-9889627-5-0

Printed in the United States
10 9 8 7 6 5 4 3 2

To the memory of Nathan Austern

Contents

Acknowledgments

MANY THANKS TO MATT CALIHMAN AND LANYA LAMOURIA for truly exceptional research assistance; and for their patient and expert guidance, I am grateful to the librarians at the Bibliothèque Nationale. Special thanks are due Willis Regier for his enthusiastic support of the project. My heartfelt thanks to Werner Sollors, who led me to Victor Séjour. I am especially grateful to Norman Shapiro, whose flawless English translation has given this play new life.

—M. Lynn Weiss

Translator's Preface

NORMAN R. SHAPIRO

WHEN I UNDERTOOK A TRANSLATION OF VICTOR SÉJOUR'S *La Tireuse de cartes* I had already completed my version of his verse drama *Diégarias*. Readers may think, understandably, that, after confronting the challenges posed by trying to put into believable and dramatically convincing English the five heroic acts of the latter, translating the prose of the former would be, as we say, "a piece of cake," and that it would virtually translate itself.

Actually, such was not the case. The challenge for a translator of theater is, obviously, to produce credible speech. Dramatic lines, being destined for recitation, are by definition much more "exposed" than passages of narrative fiction or, for that matter, even of lyric poetry. While I have often said, and willingly repeat, that all literature should, ideally, be written to be heard, the fact is that, with the exception of "talking books" for the blind (or for especially literate long-distance drivers), few readers these days hear novels read, or read them aloud themselves, or even recite them internally. And, while it is probably more common to read poetry aloud, I suspect that even with that genre most are willing to do so in silence, stopping from time to time only to share especially effective lines with a lover, a friend, or—for those of us who make our livings at it—our students. Theater, on the other hand, *has* to be heard, if not through the air, at least through the head.

Now, that being the case, why on earth would anyone find it less challenging to do a verse translation of a play than one in prose? I think the reason, in my case at any rate, is that verse, by its very nature, is an artificial medium. Characters do not go about emoting in rhymed iambic pentameter couplets in English any more than they spout alternating masculine and feminine rhymed couplets in French alexandrines, with the several prosodic constraints that traditional French versification imposes. (One could even argue that, thanks to his unrhymed verse, Shakespeare, intricacies of period language aside, is more credible in this regard than even the greatest of French classicists. But that's another matter.) The reader of a verse drama in either language, therefore, expects a certain heroic pomposity, a certain distancing from the everyday, and willingly accepts it. The translator of such into English attempts, of course, to minimize that inherent unnaturalness, and, by modulating rhythms, playing with enjambments, devising inner rhymes, breaking lines here and there, interjecting exclamations, and performing similar tricks, tries to produce a result that both respects the formal straitjacket and yet approximates believable speech. But the artificiality is, ipso facto, always there. With prose there is no similar expectation. The characters of *La Tireuse de cartes* speak the more or less standard French of Séjour's day, with an occasional nod toward the century past, and with the idiosyncratic variations of their particular station in life, as well as with moments of heightened dramatic elegance demanded by given situations. If the translator fails to make them sound natural in English, there can be no excuse, no nobility of poetic style to hide behind, no exigencies of rhyme or meter to blame for the failure.

If, however, this prose drama presents no inherent generic distancing, it does present a temporal and cultural one. While it can be argued that its characters seem to be more of Séjour's own mid-nineteenth century than of their own mid-eighteenth, they are at any rate certainly not of ours. Nor is their language, though more closely that of the play's composition than of its action. To make their dialogue natural—and, incidentally, to tailor its rhythms, its emphases, its pauses to fit comfortably on the tongues of potential Anglophone actors—the translator has to settle on a language that does not call attention to itself; one that, without going so far as to affect an English exactly contemporaneous, in every lexical and idiomatic detail, with the original French, whether itself authentically dated or not, at least avoids obvious anachronisms and sore-thumb modernisms that would immediately wrench it askew. Assuming, that is, that one wants to preserve a certain periodicity. With *La Tireuse de cartes* one hardly has a choice: since it is the fictionalized dramatization of a true historical event, it would seem ill-advised to update its setting and language to, say, the present, and still pass it off as a faithful rendition of Séjour's work rather than as an out-and-out adaptation.

Such were the basic challenges that this venture posed, obvious from the start. As so often happens, however, once I got "into the text," I found that they were not the only ones. Unlike many scenically meticulous contemporaries of his, Séjour's sometimes cavalier handling of stage directions and less-than-lucid set descriptions—the beginning of Act I is a good case in point, filled with detail but confusing in the extreme—often made it difficult to visualize the dramatic action called for, something that, as a translator, I find essential. In several instances I was obliged to be not only translator but virtual *metteur en scène* as well, suggesting ways of coping with the action's and dialogue's demands; problems that should not, ideally, be the translator's bailiwick. I likewise felt I had to tinker with the names of some of the characters: it seemed to me that, as Italians (albeit in a French play), they should all at least have Italian names, spelled *à l'italienne* and not *à la française* ("Marta," not "Marthe," "Ruccioni," not "Rutchioni," et alia). All, that is, except for the one French character, nicknamed in the original "La Pinsonnette" (the little finch), always ready to break into song, whom I took the liberty of dubbing "Mademoiselle Loriole," not only to preserve her Frenchness but also to suggest her name's ornithological and musical associations. Similarly, I felt it was only logical—and dramatically realistic—to Italianize the forms of address from *monsieur* and *madame* to *signore* and *signora*.

In short, anyone who compares my translation to Séjour's original will find what I would like to think is a balanced combination of fidelity and freedom. This is not an archival text intended to transmit literally a work of historical significance and nothing else. Minor, and on a few occasions somewhat more than minor, liberties occur at almost every turn; liberties linguistic and scenic, but all in the interest of bringing the play to life for twenty-first-century actors, spectators—and, of course, readers—alike. If it is performed, as I think it deserves to be, modern audiences will, I hope, find that, though very much a work of the past, it can, despite or perhaps thanks to those liberties, still speak very eloquently to the present and, indeed, the future.

Introduction

M. LYNN WEISS

A CURIOUS FEATURE OF NINETEENTH-CENTURY FRENCH theater history is that one of its popular playwrights was a free man of color from New Orleans, Victor Séjour. This would be remarkable for any American writer, but for a Creole of color it was extraordinary. In 1837, Séjour published "Le Mulâtre" ("The Mulatto"), the first short story by an African American.[1] In 1843, when Séjour was only twenty-six, his first play, *Diégarias* (*The Jew of Seville*), was accepted by the venerable Comédie Française.[2] Between 1844 and 1875 twenty of his twenty-two plays were produced in Paris; in one season three Séjour plays were in production simultaneously. The city's best-known drama critics reviewed his work along with that of Alexandre Dumas (père), Eugène Scribe, and Emile Augier. Napoleon III attended the premier performances of *The Fortune-Teller* and *The Syrian Massacres*. And when Séjour died in 1874, his death was reported by the *Times* (London), Reuters, *L'Abeille de la Nouvelle Orléans*, and the *New Orleans Times*.[3] To appreciate the extent of Victor Séjour's exceptional career, we need to consider where he began.

Victor Séjour was born into the Creole-of-color community of New Orleans in 1817. In the early decades of the nineteenth century, the flood of refugees from the Haitian revolution dramatically increased the population of this already prosperous community. By the 1830s, Creoles of color owned cotton and sugar plantations and some owned slaves; others worked as carpenters, printers, and iron smiths or entered professions such as medicine or education.[4] Victor Séjour's father, Louis, was a Haitian immigrant and his mother, Héloïse, was a free woman of color from New Orleans. The Séjour family lived in the Vieux Carré neighborhood, where Louis owned a small business. Séjour attended the Sainte Barbe Academy, where prosperous families of the community sent their children.[5] Like many of his peers, Victor Séjour left New Orleans between 1834 and 1836 for Paris, to complete his education. Instead, he became a remarkably successful playwright.

Louisiana's history as a French and then a Spanish territory had an important impact on the way slaves and free persons of color were perceived and treated. Evidence of this is apparent in the adaptation of the *Code noir*, a set of laws initially outlined to regulate the lives of slaves in the French colonies under Louis XIV.[6] The *Code noir*, according to historian Caryn Cossé Bell, recognized the "moral personality" of slaves inasmuch as it required that slaves be instructed in the teachings of the Catholic church and that they be baptized, married, and buried in the church. Slaves were also forbidden to work on Sundays and other Catholic holy days.[7] Indeed the origins of the racial mixture that came to be known as "Creole of color" are traceable to the early eighteenth century, when French and Spanish colonists often took slave women as mistresses or wives, freed them, and recognized and raised their children.[8] Louisiana's Creoles of color were an extraordinary exception to the general condition of free blacks in the antebellum United States. But the community became increasingly vulnerable in the decades before the Civil War. In "The Mulatto," *The Jew of Seville*, and *The Fortune-Teller*, Séjour explores the vulnerability of his "neither black nor white yet both" community in plots that feature a character who embodies, either through birth or training, both sides of a divided house.

Victor Séjour's short story "The Mulatto" was first published in 1837 in the abolitionist journal *Revue des colonies*, the organ of a radical society of people of color edited by Cyrille Auguste Bissette.[9] It is the familiar story of the white master who fathers a son he refuses to acknowledge. Years later the son, Georges, seeking revenge for his wife's death, kills his master, unaware until it is too late that this same man is his father. The horror of his crime then prompts Georges to take his own life. This theme appears repeatedly throughout the nineteenth century, in such works as Lydia Maria Child's "The Quadroons" (1842), William Wells Brown's *Clotel or: the President's Daugh-*

ter (1853), Dion Boucicault's *The Octoroon* (1859), and Charles Chesnutt's "The Sheriff's Children" (1899).[10] Séjour's tale is remarkable not only because it appears so early but because it renders the horrors of chattel slavery with economy and frankness.

Although formally very unlike "The Mulatto," *The Jew of Seville*, Séjour's first drama, revisits the tragic fate of children of mixed unions. In *The Jew of Seville*, the protagonist Diégarias is a Jew who passes as a Christian. Diégarias marries a Christian woman with whom he has a daughter. Like Georges in "The Mulatto," Inès is unaware of her father's true identity. She is also unaware that Don Juan, the man she believes is her husband, has married her in a sham ceremony. When Diégarias learns this, he demands that Don Juan lawfully marry his daughter. But Don Juan has discovered the truth about Diégarias and publicly announces that he will not marry a Jew's daughter. To retaliate, Diégarias offers the king a fortune in exchange for Don Juan's death. Inès, still in love with Don Juan, begs her father to rescind the death sentence. When he refuses, she arranges Don Juan's escape and poisons herself when it fails. In both "The Mulatto" and *The Jew of Seville*, polarized societies drive the "mixed" offspring to suicide. *The Fortune-Teller* is a variation of this theme and is based on an actual event.

In the years between the production of *The Jew of Seville* and *The Fortune-Teller*, Victor Séjour had become a very successful playwright. By 1859, eleven of his plays had been produced, some of which were so popular that they were reproduced. *Le Fils de la Nuit* (*Son of the Night*) was one of the most popular plays of the 1856 season.[11] Stylistically Séjour had moved from the classical drama of the Comédie Française to the popular theaters of the Boulevard du Temple, where the appetite of the ever-growing middle class for entertainment was constant. Some of Paris's best actors performed in Séjour's plays—Frédérick-Lemaître had the starring role in *André Gerard* and Marie Laurent played leading roles in *Le Fils de la Nuit* and *The Fortune-Teller*.[12] Reviews of Séjour's work, written by critics such as Théophile Gautier, Jules Janin, and Félix Savard, regularly appeared in the city's newspapers and theater journals. In 1859, Victor Séjour was in an excellent position to dramatize one of the most notorious instances of anti-Semitism in Italian history.

In June of 1858, the inquisitor of Bologna ordered six-year-old Edgardo Mortara removed from his Jewish family. A Christian maid who had worked for the Mortaras claimed that she had baptized the boy some years earlier during an illness from which she believed he would die. According to the church, Edgardo was now a Catholic and therefore could not be raised in a Jewish home; the church would return the boy only if the family converted to Catholicism. The hierarchy, specifically Pope Pius IX, refused to change or moderate this position throughout the parents' long campaign to recover their child. Edgardo Mortara was never returned to his family.[13]

In February of 2000, the *New York Times* reported that the Vatican had beatified Pius IX, a step in the process of officially declaring him a saint. Invoking the Mortara affair, the Italian Jewish community vehemently protested the decision.[14] Even in its own day, the Mortara case provoked an international torrent of protest against the Catholic church in general and against Pope Pius IX in particular. The affair prompted American and European Jewish communities to create civil rights organizations such as Alliance Israélite universelle, and they flooded their governments with petitions for censure and published and circulated articles on every aspect of the Mortaras' struggle.[15] In France, the Jewish newspapers *L'univers Israélite* and *Archives Israélites* petitioned Napoleon III to intervene on behalf of the Mortaras. The French, never overly fond of the Vatican (although French troops had enforced papal authority in Italy since the Garibaldi uprising of 1848–49), were appalled that their government was complicit in the whole affair.[16] Ultimately the case provided Napoleon III with the opportunity to plan and participate in the 1870 coup d'état that brought a definitive end to papal rule.[17]

In his 1997 study *The Kidnapping of Edgardo Mortara*, David Kertzer describes the numerous literary responses to the Mortara incident. Victor Séjour's *The Fortune-Teller* was immediately translated into Italian and performed in Bologna in 1860; in the same year, Herman Moos, an American, published *Mortara: Or the Pope and His Inquisitors*. In 1861 Riccardo Castelvecchio's *La famiglia ebrea* appeared. Stirling Coyne's English adaptation of *The Fortune-Teller*, entitled *The Woman in Red*, was performed in 1868 and published in 1872.[18] Even Garibaldi worked the Mortara incident into his novel, *I mille.* More recently, a novel published in 1983, *La Carrozza di San Pietro* by Pier Domiano Ori and Giovanni Perich, is based on the case.[19] Kertzer argues that *The Fortune-Teller* was the most historically significant of these numerous renditions because Napoleon attended the play's opening night, signaling the direction of France's foreign policy. And that Séjour collaborated with Jean-François-Constant Mocquard, Napoleon's private secretary, added to the political implications of the play.[20] *The Fortune-Teller* differs from other representations of the case in that Séjour makes the kidnapped Jewish infant a girl and moves the action of the play forward seventeen years.

In the prologue, Marta, a family servant and wet nurse to the infant Noémi, has already turned her over to the church and nervously awaits the return of the parents Gédéon and Géméa Ben-Meïr. Marta is pained by her decision but, in a dichotomy that formulates the conflict of the play, says: "And if the heart of a mother tells me that I've sinned, the heart of a good Christian tells me that I'm forgiven" (prologue, scene 3). Baby Noémi, now significantly called Paola, is adopted by a Christian couple, Bianca and Signore Lomellini. The names Noémi and Paola refer to archetypal conversions, from pagan to Jew and from Jew to Christian. Noémi refers to Naomi, the Jewish mother-in-law for whose sake Ruth the Moabite converts to Judaism (Ruth 2:16–17). And just as Noémi becomes Paola, Saul of Tarsus marks his conversion to Christianity by becoming Paul (Acts 9:1–19 and 13:9). But these conversion narratives underscore the difference between the voluntary act of an adult (Ruth and Saul choose their faith) and the abduction of a child, who is then reared in a faith. When Gédéon and Géméa return and learn the truth of what has happened to their daughter, their fury causes Marta to die, taking the secret of the child's whereabouts with her.

The drama begins seventeen years later; Gédéon has died and Géméa has spent the years disguised as an impoverished fortune-teller even though she is quite rich. In this guise, Géméa nurses the hope that someone's secret will lead her to her daughter. The noblewoman Bianca Lomellini has turned to the fortune-teller for a loan to pay her husband's ransom. Géméa agrees but, now certain that Paola is her daughter Noémi, she compels Bianca to reveal the truth of the young woman's origins. When Bianca confesses, Géméa goes to reclaim her daughter. This begins the bitter struggle between the mothers for Paola's heart; it will be a contest between the claims of nature and nurture and between Jew and Gentile.

Géméa begins her claim to Paola by invoking both God and the natural rights of mothers: "Nature will plead my cause for me! Nature, and my God!" (act 4, scene 8). When Marta tells her that Noémi is now a Christian, Géméa cries, "You can't tear the religion of our ancestors from a heart, and expect it not to leave its roots!" (prologue, scene 16). The power of Géméa's rhetoric is such that Bianca is compelled to employ it to argue her case. In the climatic scene where the mothers demand that Noémi/Paola choose between them, Bianca reminds her: "But I am your mother too!... She gave birth to your flesh, but I gave birth to your soul!" (act 4, scene 9). Géméa counters with the flesh-and-blood experience of having nursed her near fatally ill infant daughter back to life. In the biblical story to which this scene refers, Solomon decides to divide the contested infant in half to satisfy the rival mothers (1 Kings 3:16–28). The battle between Géméa and Bianca similarly tears Noémi/Paola apart. But just as Solomon never really knows who the infant's mother is, only which of the two women does not want him to die, the battle to decide who has the greater right to the title "mother" is a draw. Indeed, so torn by the pressure to choose between them, Noémi/Paola accuses both mothers of trying to kill her, "Every word you speak kills me! Why can you not see it? Does your love give you the right to torment my sick heart? You would have me choose to reject my God or to betray my mother! How can I? How?" (act 4, scene 9). After this outburst, the young woman descends into madness, and this brings about a truce between Bianca and Géméa. Noémi/Paola only recovers when she remembers her prayers. Ultimately she returns to Géméa but not to Judaism. In the context of the deep antagonism between the Jewish and Christian communities, Noémi/Paola's position seems untenable. Unlike Georges and Inès, Noémi/Paola does not die, but it is difficult to imagine her life.

In Séjour's rendering of the Mortara affair, in contrast to historical fact, there is a conspicuous absence of fathers; Gédéon Ben-Meïr dies early on and Bianca's husband, Signore Lomellini, is held hostage by Turkish pirates for the entire play. (Momolo Mortara was the primary force behind the movement to release his son Edgardo from the custody of the church.) The absence of the fathers parallels the absence of a criminal justice system to protect Géméa's maternal rights, because as a Jew she has no civil rights. Structuring the play so that seventeen years have elapsed between the abduction and recovery of the child eliminates the issue that was central for the Mortaras: their natural rights as parents could not be assured without the protection of law. Presenting the abducted child as a young woman enabled Séjour to criticize the church for the abduction and simultaneously mitigate that criticism by presenting us with a lovely young woman who has flourished in the Christian milieu. And that Noémi/ Paola is engaged to marry Ottavio adds to her dilemma, for not only must she leave Bianca but her fiancé too. By shifting the focus of the struggle from the civil rights of minorities to the natural rights of mothers, Séjour averted attention from the largely political crisis the Mortara affair ignited.

The Fortune-Teller opened in December of 1859 and ran until early April of 1860. Most of the critics praised the play for its passion and elegance, and everyone agreed that the formidable Marie Laurent as Géméa and Lia Félix as Paola were brilliant.[21] Even the cranky Félix Savard admitted that The Fortune-Teller was a very good drama.[22] But the critics for L'Ami de la religion and Gazette de France strongly objected to the play's implicit anti-Catholic position. The reviewer for L'Ami de la religion had several complaints: that the stage was not the place to argue current events still unresolved; that Séjour's representation of the Mortara affair distorted the actual facts of the case; that the play pleads all too eloquently the cause of Jews, who need no such defense because in France they live quite happily. He complained further that Géméa is the most eloquent and powerful character in the play, the moral superior of Bianca or Marta. Moreover, Marie Laurent's performance provoked such a frenzy of applause that he assumed that the entire audience (except him) must have been Jewish. The reviewer concluded that such an explicit attack on Christianity is an attack on France.[23] The critic for the Gazette de France marveled that the play had been approved by the censors when even the most reputable newspapers and journals were not allowed to discuss the Mortara case. More irksome was the superiority of the "oppressed Jewess over the high born Catholic lady"; in sum, the play was simplistic and excessively pro-Jewish.[24]

When the play was published, Séjour included an eloquent and well-reasoned response to this criticism. Admitting that he intended to plead the Mortara case, Séjour then insists that his criticism does not articulate an anti-Catholic position. Rather, as a Catholic he objects to the church's refusal to respect the parents' rights. He argues that the hierarchy of the church is modeled on the hierarchy of the family. Does not, he asks, this blatant disrespect for the rights of parents have a pernicious effect on the church's authority? He concludes by recalling the disastrous consequences of religious intolerance in European history. "Intolerance is a bad counselor; worse still, a deadly one. The intolerant are smitten in advance by God: not only men, but countries as well; indeed, even more so. Yesterday Italy lay dying; perhaps Spain will lie dead tomorrow. Both are struggling against the fatality of their past." On the eve of the American Civil War, Séjour might have added the United States to this list.

American Jews petitioned President James Buchanan to criticize the pope for the abduction of the Mortara child. Buchanan declined.[25] On the eve of the American Civil War, the president may have been loath to call attention to the hypocrisy such a censure would be. For two hundred and fifty years, slave mothers and fathers had been made to endure the unspeakable sorrow of having their children taken from them, a practice protected by American law.[26] *The Fortune-Teller* begs the question "can any society survive when the bonds between parents and children are violated by its customs or laws?" And in 1859, the Mortara affair must have been a stinging reminder of Louisiana's increasingly cruel laws that, by the start of the Civil War, had so reduced the rights of the Creole community as to all but dissolve the distinction between free and slave.

The work of Victor Séjour is a generous gift to African American literary history. It challenges current ideas and prescriptive assumptions about the nature of black American writing. Long before works written in English, Victor Séjour's "The Mulatto," *The Jew of Seville,* and *The Fortune-Teller* engaged the problems of a multiracial identity in a society that remains stubbornly attached to the popular fiction that it is composed of distinct groups that never cross racial boundaries. It is my hope that Norman Shapiro's brilliant translation of *The Fortune-Teller* will assure one of Louisiana's most remarkable native sons a permanent place in American literary history.

Notes

1. Victor Séjour, "Le Mulâtre," *Revue des colonies* 3, no. 9 (Mar. 1837): 376–92. Translated by Andrea Lee as "The Mulatto," in *The Multilingual Anthology of American Literature*, ed. Werner Sollors and Marc Shell (New York: New York University Press, 2000), 146–81.

2. Victor Séjour, *Diégarias* (Paris: C. Tresse, 1844). Translated by Norman Shapiro as *The Jew of Seville*, with an introduction by M. Lynn Weiss (Urbana: University of Illinois Press, 2002).

3. Charles Edwards O'Neill, *Séjour: Parisian Playwright from Louisiana* (Lafayette: Center for Louisiana Studies, University of Southwestern Louisiana, 1995), 153.

4. W. E. B. DuBois, *Black Reconstruction in America*, intro. by David Levering Lewis (1935; New York: Atheneum, 1992), 154.

5. O'Neill, *Séjour*, 2–5.

6. *Le Code noir: ou, Recueil des reglements rendus jusqu'à présent* (Paris: Prault, 1767; reprint, Basse-Terre and Fort-de-France: Société d'histoire de la Guadeloupe, 1980).

7. Caryn Cossé Bell, *Revolution, Romanticism, and the Afro-Creole Protest Tradition in Louisiana, 1718–1868* (Baton Rouge: Louisiana State University Press, 1997), 12–13; Charles Barthelemy Rousséve, *The Negro in Louisiana: Aspects of His History and His Literature* (1937; reprint, New York: Johnson Reprint Corporation, 1970), 20–22, 42.

8. Rousséve, *Negro in Louisiana*, 25.

9. Werner Sollors, *Neither Black nor White yet Both: Thematic Explorations of Interracial Literature* (New York: Oxford University Press, 1997), 164.

10. Jules Zanger, "The 'Tragic Octoroon' in Pre-Civil War Fiction," in *Interracialism: Black-White Intermarriage in American History, Literature and Law*, ed. Werner Sollors (New York: Oxford University Press, 2000), 284, n. 1.

11. O'Neill, *Séjour*, 43–47.

12. O'Neill, *Séjour*, 55–57, 71–72, 77.

13. David Kertzer, *The Kidnapping of Edgardo Mortara* (New York: Knopf, 1997).

14. Alessandra Stanley, "Italian Jews Denounce Vatican's Decision to Beatify Pius IX," *New York Times,* 28 June 2000; Peter Steinfels, "Beliefs: Long before Elian Gonzalez, There Was a Case Pitting a Powerful Pope against Jewish Parents," *New York Times,* 5 Feb. 2000. (Both articles are also available, for a price, through the *New York Times* electronic archives <http://www.nytimes.com>.)

15. Kertzer, *Kidnapping of Edgardo Mortara,* 250–52.

16. Kertzer, *Kidnapping of Edgardo Mortara,* 83–90, 118–42.

17. Kertzer, *Kidnapping of Edgardo Mortara,* 87, 261.

18. Stirling Coyne, *The Woman in Red* (London, 1872). See also Elèna Mortara, *Writing for Justice: Victor Séjour, the Kidnapping of Edgardo Mortara, and the Age of Transatlantic Emancipations* (Hanover: Dartmouth Press, 2015). This is the definitive study of the Mortara affair and Séjour's dramatic rendition of it.

19. Kertzer, *Kidnapping of Edgardo Mortara,* 252–53, 325 n. 2, 325 n. 12.

20. O'Neill, *Séjour,* 68.

21. O'Neill, *Séjour,* 71–74.

22. L. Félix Savard, "M. Victor Séjour," *La chronique litteraire* 2 (June 1862): 52.

23. Review of *La Tireuse de cartes* in *L'Ami de la religion* 3 (Jan. 1860): 1–2 and 3 (Mar. 1860): 1. Quoted in Era Brisbane Young, "An Examination of Selected Dramas of Victor Séjour Including Works of Social Protest" (Ph.D. diss., New York University, 1979), 161–63. Young indicates that the author of this piece was J. M. Tiengou. O'Neill cites Tiengou as the author of the review for *Gazette de France,* whereas Young indicates that the author of the *Gazette* review is M. Bornier.

24. Young, "Examination of Selected Dramas of Séjour," 163–64. Review of *La Tireuse de cartes* in *La Gazette de France* 9 (Jan. 1860): 1.

25. Kertzer, *Kidnapping of Edgardo Mortara,* 127.

26. Kertzer, *Kidnapping of Edgardo Mortara,* 127.

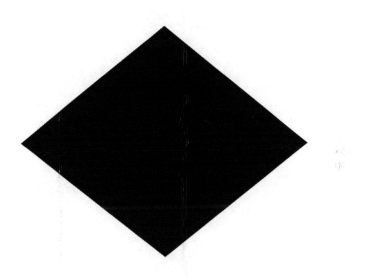

First performed at the Théâtre de la Porte Saint-Martin, 22 December 1859, with the following cast:

CHARACTERS IN THE PROLOGUE	ACTORS	
Ruccioni	Messrs.	Vannoy
Gédéon Ben-Meïr		Charly
A Doctor		E. Capon
Géméa	Mmes.	Marie-Laurent
Marta		Cornélie
Loriole		Darty
Ottavio, a five-year-old child	Mlle.	Esther

The action takes place in Bisagno, in 1728

CHARACTERS IN THE PLAY	ACTORS	
Ruccioni	Messrs.	Vannoy
Ottavio Salviati, Count Doriani		Laray
Frigolini		Bousquet
Frimagusta		Mercier
Castara		Caliste
Luppo		Josse
The First Doctor		Borsat
The Second Doctor		Alexis-Louis
The Third Doctor		E. Capon
Géméa	Mmes.	Marie-Laurent
Paola		Lia-Félix
Bianca		Suzanne-Lagier
Loriole		Darty
Catarina		Lagrange
Teresa		Morin
Pepitta	Mlle.	Camille
The First Woman		
The Second Woman		
The Third Woman		
Two Monks		
Villagers		

The action takes place in Genoa, in 1745.

———

L'Ami de la religion and *La Gazette de France* have, with the same passion and violent style, though not with the same force of logic, attacked *La Tireuse de cartes.* For the one, it is a diabolical work; for the other, an insignificant one. Both agree, however, that my salvation is in doubt.

I should like to explain myself, and I ask to be permitted to speak—only in my own name—and to profess my thoughts as succinctly as I am able.

In writing *La Tireuse de cartes,* did I desire to plead the Mortara family's cause? Clearly, I did. Did I seek to produce a diatribe against the Pope or the clergy, against Christianity, which is my faith, or Catholicism, which is my practice? Clearly, I did not. But I am a man; one of those human beings who feel that humanity revolves about the sacred tradition of the family, and who place the father under the hand of God.

One has a right to speak out loudly in defense of the desecrated home: founded on the child, that great and touching phenomenon of life; maintained by the father, that most august of authorities; blessed by the mother, God's most glorious emanation.

Is it possible that the Pope—holy man, sacred man, blessèd man that he is—might himself be in the forefront of a cruelly inhumane action? Is the cross that he bears not the symbol of brotherhood; the throne the he occupies, not the refuge from injustice? How can one protect petty and banal persecution behind this supreme embodiment of divine right? How can one debase that sanctity by dragging it into the lists, amid protests of moral rectitude, in a flurry of public conscience voiced quivering with conviction?... Do you not feel that, here, in the middle of the nineteenth century, such a stance is tactless, to say the very least? Do you not feel that the flag you are waving might be shamed in defeat and never glorious again in victory?

I am not a politician, nor am I a romantic. But the heart too can have its revelations and can rise to the lucid visions of an idea. How many problems might be resolved if only one would heed it? You steal a child from his father, and I tell you: "That is frightful!" You wrench him from the arms of his mother, and I tell you: "That is villainous!" Not only for them, but for you as well. The family is society cast small, just as humanity is the State cast large. To tamper with the one is a danger; with the other, a crime. Every event has its place, relentlessly set in the skein of human life. By approving this attack on the right of a father; by accepting, as head of the Church, this violation of the family's domain, does the Pope not invite us to question his very infallibility, and to justify the social sanction that one would impose upon him?

A pope is father to the faithful, as a father is pope to his children. I beg you to reflect. Intolerance is a bad counselor; worse still, a deadly one. The intolerant are smitten in advance by God: not only men, but countries as well; indeed, even more so. Yesterday Italy lay dying; perhaps Spain will lie dead tomorrow. Both are struggling against the fatality of their past. Their laws bespeak chaos; their authority bespeaks confusion. The world looks upon them and cannot understand. In the end, in a final, profound effort to refashion themselves, what will these two lands of the Inquisition become; these two lands that seek their own conscience in the conscience of others, and that waver now in the throes of Europe's twofold upheaval, betwixt the temptation of despotism and the attractive force of freedom?

—V.S.

Prologue

A large room in the home of Géméa. Bundles of merchandise, piled up in disorder about the room. Stage left, a staircase leading upstairs; up right, an angled corner with an open window, through which can be seen, a short distance across the way, a balcony covered with a flowering vine. Upstage center, a door. Another door, down left. Midstage left, a cradle; midstage right, a chair. Other furniture *ad libitum*.

At rise, Loriole can be seen on the balcony, embroidering and singing. Marta is seated, right, dressing Ottavio.

SCENE I
Marta, Ottavio, Loriole

Ottavio: You mean, Noémi isn't coming back?... (*Marta heaves a sigh.*) I'll never see my little sister again?

Marta (*aside*):   Heaven help me!... (*Getting up, in a whisper*) That cradle... I can't bear to look at it! (*She goes over to it and covers it with a blanket.*) It reminds me of a tomb! (*She goes to the window, calling out.*) Loriole! I'm waiting... How much longer...?

Loriole (*from the balcony*):   Right away... I'm almost done.

(*She continues her embroidery and her singing. Marta finishes dressing Ottavio.*)

Ottavio: I liked little Noémi!

Marta: Please! Her name is Paola now.

Ottavio: It is?... But why, mamma? (*Marta turns aside and sighs.*) And anyway, I miss her!

5

Marta: Quiet! You talk too much!

Ottavio: Besides, why are you getting me all dressed up? Does this week have two Sundays?

Marta (putting her finger to her lips):   Shhh!

(Ruccioni enters, upstage.)

SCENE 2
Marta, Ottavio, Loriole, Ruccioni

Ruccioni (going to the window, pointing to Loriole):   Ah! What a voice!

Marta (surprised at his entrance):   Oh!

Ottavio (turning to him):   What are you doing here?

Marta: Is that you, Signor Ruccioni?

Ruccioni: In the flesh, lovely lady... *(Gazing out at Loriole, enraptured)* Those high notes! Those trills!... It's enough to make you climb the stairs four at a time, by God!... Ah! A bird among the flowers! *(To Marta)* And your health, signora? You're well, I see?

Marta (rather wistfully):   Yes... Quite...

Ruccioni (to Ottavio, chucking him under the chin):   And you, little soldier? *(Aside, looking toward the balcony)* Ah! She almost turned this way... *(Reveling in the thought)* The street is so narrow, you could almost jump across!... *(To Marta)* Is there anything for rent here, signora? Two by four, I don't care... As long as it looks out on the street!

Marta: I'm afraid not... *(To Ottavio)* Now run along and play.

Ruccioni (to Ottavio):   Oh, don't we look fine!

6

Ottavio: May I go up and see Mademoiselle Loriole, mamma?

Ruccioni: Loriole?... Now there's a pretty name for you!

Ottavio: Mamma calls her that... Because she's French, and she's always singing... Like a bird.

Ruccioni (taking his hand, moving toward the door, upstage):   Come, I'll take you. We'll go together...

Ottavio (resisting):   No! Only if I can ride on your shoulders!

Ruccioni: No sooner said than done! (*He crouches down to let Ottavio mount.*) Here... And then, "gee up, gee up"...

Marta (as Ottavio begins to climb on his shoulders):   Ottavio!

Ottavio: But I want to see how fast he can gallop, mamma!

Ruccioni: Like the wind! You'll see!... (*Still crouching*) Come...

Marta (to Ottavio):   But mademoiselle is coming here... In just a few minutes... Now please, run along. I have to speak with the gentleman.

Ottavio (grumbling):   Oh... Just when he wants to play with me...

(*He exits, left, up the stairs.*)

SCENE 3
Ruccioni, Marta

Ruccioni: That's a handsome son you've got there, signora! And a lovely neighbor, if you don't mind my saying!

Marta (putting some things of Ottavio's into a trunk, looking toward the window):   Mademoiselle?

———
7

Ruccioni (nodding):   Loriole...

Marta: Yes... She's been here three days, but I've known her for years.

Ruccioni: Fresh as a daisy... Happy as a bird... And I'll bet she has butterfly wings, too, that angel?

Marta (emphasizing her intent):   She's a good girl, signore.

Ruccioni: Good? (*Hands together, looking heavenward, with a little sigh*) Ah... What a shame! She'll fly off to heaven, and leave me suffering here on earth! (*Looking out the window, aside*) "Good"?... I wonder... (*Aloud*) Are you packing, signora?

Marta: I'm sending Ottavio to his father.

Ruccioni: To Salviati? But... I thought he was at sea. Isn't he the boatswain's mate on *The Jupiter?*

Marta (as she continues packing):   He is, but it doesn't sail until tonight. Loriole is taking the child to the ship.

Ruccioni: Oh? And wouldn't you like me to go along too? I have nothing to do all day... My time is yours.

Marta: You're too kind, my friend. In fact...

Ruccioni: Please...

Marta: Well, if you're sure...

Ruccioni: Yours to command, mine to obey!

Marta: Very well. Then I'd like you to go the Convent of the Annunciation.

Ruccioni (taken aback):   To the... (*Aside*) Damn!

Marta: You'll take the mother superior a dress for baby Paola, and a medal that I'm going to give you... (*To herself, sadly*) Dear little thing!... (*To Ruccioni, sighing*) Ah! You don't spend a year and a half with a babe in your arms... A poor, innocent child, all hugs and smiles... You don't give her your breast, and feed her your milk, and not become attached to her. Believe me...

Ruccioni: Oh, I do...

Marta: And I have to keep saying it, again and again! Because that's my excuse!

Ruccioni: Yours, maybe... (*Clapping his hands to his chest*) But not mine!... Besides, we both had the only excuse we needed. We did what we had to do... We snatched from the clutches of two heathens, two heretics—

Marta (interrupting):   Don't talk like that!... It wasn't greed that brought me here to nurse their child, but gratitude. I'll always be grateful for what they did for me... Even more... I'll always love them for it.

Ruccioni: Those two?

Marta (continuing):   And if the heart of a mother tells me that I've sinned, the heart of a good Christian tells me that I'm forgiven.

(*Ottavio appears at the head of the staircase and begins coming down.*)

Ottavio: Forward, march!... One, two, one, two...

Marta (to Ruccioni):   I'm going to get the medal. (*Passing the window as she crosses left, to the staircase, calling to Loriole*) Please, Loriole! We're waiting!

Loriole (*getting up*):   Coming... Coming...

(*She leaves the balcony and disappears into her quarters, as Marta exits up the stairs.*)

SCENE 4
Ruccioni, Ottavio

Ruccioni (*to Ottavio, who is continuing his march across the room, standing in front of him and barring his way*):   So, you know Mademoiselle Loriole, do you?

Ottavio: Of course I do! She's mamma's friend, don't you know? (*He begins marching again.*) One, two, one, two...

Ruccioni (*holding him back*):   And she lives by herself, I suppose?

Ottavio: Of course she does, silly! She's an orphan!... You know what that is?... Oh, you couldn't know. You're too old... It's when you don't have your mamma any more. That's what an orphan is...

Ruccioni: But maybe she has a brother or two... Or a cousin... A nice little cousin, with a long mustache, maybe?

Ottavio: What for? Why should she?

Ruccioni (*aside*):   Not too big, I hope! (*Aloud, holding up his palm, waist high*) About so big?

Ottavio: Should I go ask mamma?

Ruccioni: No...

Ottavio: I will! I will!...

Ruccioni: No, I said!... (*Trying to change the subject*) So, you want to be a soldier, do you?

Ottavio: What do you care!

(*Loriole can be heard singing, off right. Ottavio runs to meet her as she enters, upstage.*)

SCENE 5
Ruccioni, Ottavio, Loriole

Ruccioni (aside): Ah! Even more ravishing up close!

Ottavio (to Loriole): Mademoiselle Loriole... (*Pointing to Ruccioni*) You don't have a brother, do you?

Loriole: No... Why?

Ottavio: Or a cousin?... (*Holding his palm up over his head, at the height where Ruccioni's had been*) So big? With a long mustache?

Loriole (with a little laugh): Not even!... But why—

Ottavio (to Ruccioni): See? (*To Loriole*) Tell him!... (*To Ruccioni*) I told you!

Ruccioni (to Ottavio, in a whisper): Quiet! (*With a little bow, to Loriole, embarrassed*) Mademoiselle... (*Mumbling*) I... I was only asking because... I assure you...

Loriole (to Ruccioni, with a little curtsy, hardly listening): Signore... (*To Ottavio, giving him a kiss*) Go tell your mamma I'm here, Ottavio.

(*Ottavio exits, up the stairs.*)

Ruccioni (aside): Could that be a "thank you" kiss, I wonder?

SCENE 6
Ruccioni, Loriole

Ruccioni (watching as Ottavio disappears): Little devil!... (*To Loriole*) Mademoiselle...

Loriole: But why should I have a brother?... Or a cousin?

Ruccioni: You shouldn't!... That is... I was hoping you didn't! I thought I might like to come pay you a visit.

Loriole (very proper): My door opens only to my friends, signore. To people I know, and who know me...

Ruccioni: But I do!... I do know you!... I've been lying in the burning sun for three days, just watching you, listening to you... Every dog in the street thinks my legs are tree stumps! Children point at me and laugh! They think I'm mad!

Loriole: Could they be right?

Ruccioni: Mad?... Yes, about you!

Loriole: My, my! A lovely pastime, I must say! Lying in the sun and watching young ladies... Have you no profession, my friend?... No trade?...

Ruccioni: I'm looking for one... Something I can do without working...

(*He stops, trying to judge her reaction.*)

Loriole: Please, go on... You amuse me.

Ruccioni: I'll tell you the rest while I see you to your door... And when we go inside...

Loriole: I told you... My door opens only to people I know... (*Rather coyly*) And to possible husbands.

Ruccioni: Perfect! Why not me? That's one profession I'm sure I can master!

Loriole (*laughing*):   Ah, but it's not that easy, I'm afraid! The man I choose will cross my threshold three times. The first, because he loves me... The second, to sign the marriage contract... And the third, when we go to the church...

Ruccioni: Hmm... Only three? (*Aside, as Marta appears at the head of the stairs*) It's not going to be as easy as I thought!

SCENE 7
Ruccioni, Loriole, and Marta

Marta (*coming down the stairs*):   Ah! Loriole!... (*As Loriole hands her a little package*) Finally... (*To Ruccioni, handing him the package, and a medal, hanging from a chain*) Here!... And be sure to give her a big hug and a kiss for me.

Ruccioni (*intentionally misunderstanding, pointing to Loriole*):   Her?... With pleasure...

Marta: Paola, signore!

Ruccioni: Of course... Of course... (*With a little bow, to Marta and Loriole*) Lovely ladies...

(*He goes to leave, upstage. As he passes in front of Loriole, he pauses for a moment and discreetly gives the back of his hand a suggestive kiss in her direction, then exits.*)

Marta, Loriole

Loriole (*to Marta, who continues packing*):   Your friend is quite the Bohemian, love!... I must say, he seems like rather a happy-go-lucky scoundrel.

Marta: Indeed...

Loriole: I didn't get his name...

Marta: Ruccioni... (*Pointing*) Pass me the shirts, please... (*As Loriole complies, packing them away and closing the trunk*) There!... (*Wiping away a tear*) So, Loriole... You're sure I can count on you?

Loriole: Really! What a question! (*With a little pirouette*) Just look at me! All decked out and ready to sail! I said to myself: "No harm in taking advantage of the occasion to primp up a little."

Marta: Yes, I see... Just look at you!

Loriole (*modestly*):   Well...

Marta (*returning to the matter at hand*):   So... It's perfectly clear. You're not to leave Ottavio with—

Loriole (*finishing her sentence*):   ... with anyone but his father! And if his father isn't there, I'm to bring him right back.

Marta: Exactly.

Loriole (*hesitating*):   Only... I can't help wondering, love... How will you bear it, being without him? How can you send him away like this? (*As Marta utters an almost inaudible sigh*) Surely it can't be that... God forgive me for even thinking it!... But it can't be that you want to give all your time to that baby girl you're nursing... That vile Jew-child!... You're too attached to her already!

Marta: Please, Loriole... You don't understand. When my own baby died... My own little girl, her foster sister...

Loriole: I know... I know...

Marta: All the love that I felt... All the tenderness in my heart... I simply gave it all to her... Dear little things! You can never love them enough!

Loriole: It would seem that her own mother doesn't quite agree!

Marta: That's not true. She adores her.

Loriole (with a touch of sarcasm):   No doubt!... Perhaps that's why she left her here, to go running off to Napoli... (*As Marta is about to object*) I'm only repeating what I've heard... That's right, Napoli... For some inheritance or other... Both of them... The husband and the wife... Waiting for his millionaire uncle to die... And, in the meantime, their own child, here, was almost dead herself... Why, if not for you, love, they would come back and find her lying in the grave!

Marta (emphasizing):   If not for God, Loriole...

Loriole: God?

Marta: Paola had been sick for three days... I told you... Fever, convulsions... The doctors had given her up for dead. Then, on the fourth day... A dark, dismal day... (*Pointing to the chair*) I can still see myself sitting there, alone, in that chair, with that poor child on my lap. Her arms and legs were all twisted in pain... Her eyes were clouded... And all I could do was sit there, powerless, too weary to move... Just sit there and watch her dying, dying... Not even able to shed a tear... But I must have been praying! Yes, praying, Loriole... I'm sure I must have been, because I never lost hope. Not for a minute... And the hours went by... My little Ottavio was sleeping by my side... Suddenly, without thinking, I turned and looked at him. A medal of the Virgin was hanging from his neck... I see it beckoning to me, and I take it... I place it on the heart of that suffering little child... Lovingly, gently... And all at once, Loriole... Oh, joy!... All at once that heart that has all but stopped beating comes pounding back to life! Those frigid lips begin to move... A smile, Loriole... A smile like an angel's comes over that deathly face! It was life!... The breath of life, in that little body... And I got up... It was as if heaven was sending me a message... I got up and I dipped my hand in the holy water... And I made the sign of the cross on her forehead, and said the sacred words... I had barely even finished, when she opened her eyes, and I swear she leaned her little blond head toward me, as if to thank me...

Loriole (*who has been listening in rapt attention*):   Oh!...

Marta (*continuing*):   Oh, Loriole, how can I tell you the feeling that came over me? How can I explain my soul's yearning for God? It was a miracle... I knew it, I could see it, I could touch it!... And I said to myself: "I must sanctify this act! It's the will of God!" So I took the child in my arms, and I ran to the convent...

Loriole: You didn't!

Marta: Out in the street, I found a man lying in the sun, looking up at your balcony. "Come quick!" I shouted, and I tugged him by the arm. He got up and followed me. Ten minutes later the child was reborn, ready to live a life in Christ. They gave her the name Paola. The man was your Signore Ruccioni. He was her godfather... I was her godmother.

Loriole (*incredulous*):   You dared...?

Marta: It was only then that I realized what it meant... Now that she was a Christian, she had to be raised by Christians!

Loriole: And...?

Marta: She had to leave this house!

Loriole: Oh! Marta, love! What have you done?

Marta: My duty...

Loriole: But... When they come back... (*Realizing the danger*) Quick! Where is Ottavio? I must take him away! Who knows what they might do?

Marta: Her father may kill me! I'm sure he'll try... The fever that wracks him will make his blood boil, and he'll lash out against me...

Loriole (*appalled*):   No!

Marta: But then it will pass. He'll not be the one to suffer.

Loriole: And Géméa?

Marta: Ah, yes... Géméa, poor soul!... When I think how desperate, how distraught she'll be... Oh! I could loathe myself for what I've done!... When I think how the poor woman struggles to survive, how she trudges from Bisagno to Genova, peddling her wares... From Genova to Torino... And now, when she'll come home, at the end of a grueling day, she'll not even have her daughter's smile to calm her and ease her pain!... (*Pointing to the cradle*) How often have I seen her there, all through the night, watching the child sleep!... Motionless as a statue... Tender, afraid to move, afraid she might wake her... Crouching by the cradle, her eyes glowing like a beast's... Not a woman, not a mother... A wolf, Loriole! A she-wolf protecting, watching over her young!

Loriole (*with a shudder*):   Good heavens!... And you've taken her baby?... This she-wolf, as you call her?... And you're waiting for her, here? And... And you'll admit it?

Marta: Yes.

Loriole: But how? What?... What will you tell them?

Marta (*simply*):   The truth.

Loriole: Please!... At least you could tell them that she's dead!... That she died...

Marta: I would be lying.

Loriole: Then let me tell them. I'll lie! I don't mind...

Marta: I would be just as guilty if I didn't deny it.

Loriole: Then... Then leave! Run away!

Marta: I'll not abandon their house to marauders.

Loriole: But, my God! Marta, love... This is madness!... Don't forget, you're still nursing... Your milk... The least little shock, and your milk could choke you!... Please! It could kill you! Think what you're doing...

Marta: My life is in God's hands.

Loriole: Even worse, it could drive you mad...

Marta: I'll be strong.

Loriole: But how can you be sure?

Marta: At least, I'll do my best... (*Eager to change the subject*) Come, we must think of Ottavio... (*Going to the window, calling*) Pietro!... Come up please!... (*Wiping away a tear, as she checks the trunk one more time*) Everything is there...

(*Pietro enters, upstage.*)

Pietro (*with a little bow to Marta and then to Loriole*):   Signora... Signorina...

Marta (*to Pietro, pointing*):   The trunk, Pietro... Take it down and put it in old Giovanni's wagon. (*To Loriole*) I paid him for it... (*To Pietro*) It's just outside the door. (*To Loriole, sighing*) You'll tell Salviati that I'll come see him tomorrow, first thing. But mind you, not another word! He would worry if he knew... (*Calling*) Ottavio!... Ottavio!...

(*As Pietro leaves with the trunk, Ottavio comes running down the stairs. She takes him in her arms and covers him with kisses.*)

SCENE 9
Marta, Loriole, Ottavio

Ottavio: Why are you hugging me so hard, mamma?

Marta: No reason...

Ottavio: And you're crying!

Marta (*forcing a smile*):   Nothing of the kind!

Ottavio: Oh! That's naughty, mamma! You always tell me not to lie, and now you're lying!

Marta (*turning her head, to Loriole*):   Take him, Loriole...

Ottavio: Where, mamma? Where is Mademoiselle Loriole taking me?

Loriole (*trying to sound cheerful*):   To your father, precious...

Ottavio (clapping his hands):   Oh! Am I going to see his ship? Am I going to?... Am I? Am I?

Loriole: Of course you are!

Ottavio: Then hurry up! (*Tugging at her arm*) Don't be so slow!...

(*He and Loriole leave, upstage, as Marta, reaching out in a gesture of separation, watches sadly.*)

SCENE 10
Marta, alone

Marta: It's done!... And I'm alone!... (*Looking about the room*) Alone, amid all this disorder and confusion... Like the picture of my mind!... (*Shaking her head*) Alone, with my despair... (*She moves among the bundles of merchandise piled here and there.*) But soon she'll be here too... That poor woman... That childless mother!... (*She places her hand against her brow in a gesture of despair.*) Good God!... (*Picking up articles of the baby's clothing*) Ah!... Her bonnet... Her little shoes... One day they'll be like so many holy relics! (*She puts them in the cradle.*) She'll find them... Here, in this empty cradle!... (*She stops and listens, as she hears footsteps coming up the stairs, outside.*) Already? God help me, they're here...

(*Ruccioni enters, upstage.*)

SCENE 11
Marta, Ruccioni

Marta: You!... (*With a sigh of relief*) Thank heaven!... I thought... (*To herself*) That smell of death...

Ruccioni (downcast):   Signora...

Marta: Well? Did you see her?

Ruccioni: Ah! I'm glad I didn't let myself grow too attached...

Marta: Why? What do you mean...?

Ruccioni (shaking his head): Tsk tsk tsk... Some people... (*Sighing*) Some people are born to go through life... Through all eternity... Like animals, with no purpose, no reason for being... Trapped in their meaningless, lonely existence...

Marta: My friend...?

Ruccioni: If they're hungry they grab something in their paws and eat... If people tease them they reach out their claws and give them a swipe... (*As Marta looks at him quizzically*) Ah! That child, signora... I know that, just with that look of hers... Her eyes, her smile... I know that she could have made me a man, given me a reason... I could have devoted my life to her! My life...

Marta: But...

Ruccioni (with a gesture, shaking his head): Pfff!... Gone!

Marta (taken aback): Gone?

Ruccioni: They gave her a pair of wings, and the angel has flown away!

Marta (alarmed): What?... What do you mean?

Ruccioni: Mean?... I mean that the mother superior didn't waste any time... Oh, she's a fine woman, don't misunderstand... When I got there she was in the dormitory, with Paola in her arms, walking back and forth... Muttering, grumbling... And shaking the child like a plum-tree to make her stop crying...

Marta: Was she ill?

Ruccioni: The mother superior?

Marta (impatiently): Paola, for goodness' sake!... Paola!

Ruccioni: No, no... All of a sudden she turns around, slips the child in my arms, and goes running off.

Marta: But...

Ruccioni: There I am, not knowing what to do... Muttering and grumbling too, you can imagine!... But then she looks at me... And she knows me! And she smiles!... She smiles at me, signora! And it was all so sudden that... Would you believe it? I began to weep... Tears of joy... Like a fool, I know... But after all, I'm her godfather! I had the right to cry a little, didn't I?

Marta: My friend...

Ruccioni: And I'm standing there, trying to explain it all to her, as if she could understand... Next thing I know, she closes her eyes and falls asleep.

Marta: But... The mother superior...?

Ruccioni: In a minute or two she comes back with a woman... A real lady, by the looks of her... (*With a grand gesture from head to toe*) All fancy... With a thick veil on her face... And she takes the child, and they motion me to get out... Well, when I'm in a holy place I don't argue! But a little while later I went back in... The mother superior was standing in a corner, all alone, with a smile all over her face.

Marta: And Paola...?

Ruccioni: That's what I said... "What about Paola?" And she tells me: "Her new mother has taken her... Adopted her, signore... And she's sworn to love her like her very own daughter, and to raise her as a Christian..."

Marta: "Taken her..."? But... Where?

Ruccioni: She wouldn't tell me. I think it's a secret...

Marta: But... That can't be! It's impossible!

Ruccioni: That's what I said... "That's impossible!" I yelled... And just to let her know how I felt... (*Crossing himself*) God forgive me!... I threw in one of my strongest curses!... And she jumped back like... Well, you'd think a snake had just nipped at her toes!... "Out, you...!" she screams, and she points to the door... I was so ashamed, signora, I slipped out like a breeze... And here I am!... (*Marta hurriedly puts on her cloak.*) Where are you going?

Marta: To the convent!... (*Agitated*) When I left her they promised I could always see her!... And now her mother is coming back, and... Oh! What will I tell her?... Good God! It's impossible!... No! It can't be...

(*She goes to leave, upstage.*)

Ruccioni: Wait!... The lady left thirty crowns... "For the godparents," the mother superior told me... (*Counting*) Fifteen for the godfather... (*He pockets them.*) And fifteen for the godmother...

(*He holds them out to her, tentatively.*)

Marta (*waving him off*): Please! You keep them!...

(*She leaves.*)

SCENE 12
Ruccioni, alone

Ruccioni: Now that's one fine woman!... I'd never be that generous, but I'm glad she is!... I can see why, too, at a time like this... (*Jingling the coins*) Oh well, that's fifteen crowns more and five hun-

---

23

gry days less!... So much the better!... Good luck has some time now to go visit someone else...

(*Loriole enters, upstage.*)

SCENE 13
Ruccioni, Loriole

Loriole (*to Ruccioni*):   Is my friend here?

Ruccioni: She just left, lovely lady! She went to the convent... But don't go... She'll be back...

Loriole (*hardly paying attention, obviously upset*):   Yes... I see...

Ruccioni: Is something wrong, mademoiselle? If you don't mind my asking...

Loriole: Oh! It's nothing... Really... It's... It's just that, a moment ago... Outside... An unspeakable ragamuffin insulted me... (*Pointing*) Out there...

Ruccioni (*gallantly*):   Where? I'll kill the blackguard! I swear I will!!... Where is he?

Loriole: No... Please!... (*Becoming calm*) He called me a vile name, that's all... One that I should be accustomed to by now...

Ruccioni: Oh?

Loriole: A "bastard"!!... That's what he called me...

Ruccioni: Ah?... Well, Mademoiselle Loriole, at least that's one thing we have in common! I was a foundling too, I'll have you know... Some say I was found in a field, some say it was on a road outside the village... But they all agree that it was a freezing cold day, and that I was starving!

Loriole: How dreadful!...

Ruccioni: Mothers who abandon their babies, mademoiselle... Ah! If they could only realize what they're doing!... It's one thing if they die. After all, where's the harm?... A hole in the ground and a prayer, and that's the end of it!... But if they don't... If they're strong, if they survive... Despite hunger, and cold, and the carts rolling by... Despite the drunkard that stumbles and tramples them half to death... Ah! (*Sarcastically*) What a fine breed of men and women they become!... Men with no one to love, and who can only hate... Men scorned, who live for vengeance... Men stalked, who live to kill!...

Loriole (*touched*):   How awful...

Ruccioni: The day they hang me... (*Loriole shudders.*) Oh yes, mademoiselle, it can happen, believe me! Even to the best, most upright among us... That day, my mother may be in the crowd, watching... Maybe even clapping... Not suspecting for a moment that a smile by the cradle, a simple kiss, and it never would have happened... Poor thing!... To hide a sin, see all the crimes she bred!

Loriole: Oh...

Ruccioni (*abruptly changing the subject*):   Where were you born, Loriole?

Loriole: In France... Paris... In 1712...

Ruccioni: And me, in 1706... In the Apennines, between Frasinone and Ytry... We're kin in misfortune, you and I.

(*He holds out his hand to her.*)

Loriole (*grasping it*):   Brother...

Ruccioni (*warmly*):   Sister... Promise me you'll never abandon a child!

(As they stand for a long moment in silence, the door, upstage, opens and Marta enters, pale and shaken.)

SCENE 14
Loriole, Ruccioni, Marta

Ruccioni (turning to her, surprised):   Signora!...

Marta (to Loriole, looking about):   Good! Ottavio isn't with you...

Loriole: No, love... I delivered him to Salviati in person!... Just as you said... (*Jovially*) And he told me to give you a hug and a kiss for him!... (*Embracing her*) There!

Marta (aside):   Thank God! At least he'll be safe... (*To Ruccioni*) I know where they've taken Paola, my friend...

Ruccioni: Ah...

Loriole (to Ruccioni, quizzically):   "Taken" her?... But she's in the convent...

Marta (as Ruccioni explains the situation, sotto voce, to Loriole):   And I had to swear on my honor never to tell the name of the lady...

Loriole (to Ruccioni, aghast):   Adopted?... (*To Marta*) Good heavens!

Marta (continuing):   Or where she lives, or anything about her... (*To Ruccioni*) Never! Not even if I'm tortured!... Besides, she's leaving in a month and taking Paola with her.

Loriole: Poor Marta! What a shock!... And I've just learned that her mother is back from Napoli... The Jewess!

Marta: Géméa?

Loriole: And Ben-Meïr too... Even weaker than before!... Some peddlars saw them on the road... He could scarcely walk, they said... Even with his fancy stick, and clinging to her arm...

Marta: Poor soul...

Loriole: But she couldn't wait to see her child, so she left him behind and hurried on ahead.

Marta (sighing):   Of course...

Loriole: And they told me that the uncle finally died, and they've inherited their millions!

Ruccioni (sarcastically):   Good! That should console them!

Marta (to Ruccioni):   Not a mother, my friend! You think mothers have no feelings?

Ruccioni: Which ones? (*Cynically*) The ones who abandon their babies? Or the ones who sell them... Who leave them, and go running after gold?

Marta: Please...

Ruccioni: And what does it matter? Her mother was a fortune-teller... If she passed on her art, the Jewess is sure to find her daughter one day!

Loriole (to Marta, tenderly):   We'll stay with you if you like...

Marta: No... God and my conscience are on my side. Now it's mother to mother... Best you leave me alone, and let me collect my thoughts.

Loriole: As you wish, love... (*To Ruccioni*) Come...

(*She and Ruccioni leave, upstage.*)

SCENE 15
Marta, alone

Marta: Yes... God and my conscience! He commanded and I
obeyed... At least, so I thought... Then what have I to fear? He'll
place His will before me, like a shield, to protect me. And He'll
calm the distress of this poor, desperate mother!... (*Shuddering*)
Oh!... (*Looking around the room*) Everything is in order... (*She sits
in the chair.*) If I've sinned... If I've transgressed the divine laws of
heaven, His punishment will be clear!... (*Listening*) Ah!... Footsteps... So quick... It must be... (*She crosses herself, as the door, upstage, flies open.*) God help me!... It is...

(*She clutches her cloak around her as Géméa enters, breathless.*)

SCENE 16
Marta, Géméa

Géméa: Ah, Marta, Marta!... (*Removing her cape, trying to catch her
breath*) My dear, dear Marta... I simply couldn't wait! I left poor
Ben-Meïr behind and came as fast as I could! (*Sighing*) Oh... I
thought it would take forever!... (*Approaching her*) My baby... My
Noémi... How is she?

Marta: She's...

Géméa (*without waiting for a reply*): Poor darling!... Is she sleeping?...
Shhh! Shhh!... I'll not make a sound... I only want to kiss her!

Marta (*holding her back*): No!

Géméa: You're right... What's the hurry? Now that I'm finally here...
And our child is rich, Marta... Worth millions... (*Pointing to the
cradle*) Why, her cradle... That cradle that holds my whole reason
for being... That cradle that holds my life is too small to hold her
fortune! (*Gazing lovingly at the cradle*) Oh! How I ache to see her...
To give her a little kiss... How I've hungered, how I've yearned!...

No! I can't wait!... (*Marta gives a start.*) Just imagine, a month... One whole month since I've laid eyes on her!... Did she call me? Did she look for me?... Has she grown?... Oh! I have to...

(*She tiptoes over to the cradle, holding her breath.*)

Marta (*aside*):   Poor soul...

Géméa (*gently pulling the covers, shocked*):   She... She isn't here!... Marta, she... Where...? Where is she?

Marta: Signora...

Géméa (*as if struck by a realization*):   Ah! Of course!... You've put her in my bed!... Dear, dear Marta!... How thoughtful of you... The air is so much better upstairs...

(*She hurries up the staircase and disappears.*)

Marta: Good God!

Géméa (*appearing*):   She's not here! She... But... (*Hurrying down the stairs*) But where is she, Marta?... My Noémi... Where is she?... (*Going up to her, suddenly smiling*) Oh! Naughty, naughty!... (*Pointing to Marta, who is still clutching her cloak about her*) You're holding her in your arms! My treasure... (*Reaching out*) Let me have her... (*Pulling the cloak aside, and jumping back, with a shriek*) Ahhh!... She... She's dead, isn't she?... My Noémi is dead!... That's what you're trying tell me!

Marta (*trying to calm her*):   No... No, please...

Géméa: No?... Then why are you so pale?

Marta (*standing up, looking aside*):   Your child is alive, believe me...

Géméa: Then look me in the eye! If you want me to believe you...

Marta: She's alive, I swear... But...

Géméa (growing frantic): God of Abraham, Isaac, and Jacob!...
What is she going to tell me? What disaster...

Marta: She's lost...

Géméa: Lost?... How?... Where?

Marta: Lost to you...

Géméa: Lost to me...?

Marta: I had to save her!

Géméa: What? From some danger?... From... Tell me! Tell me!

Marta: From death!

Géméa: My child? My Noémi?

Marta: The doctors gave her up... There was nothing they could
do...

Géméa: And you saved her? You...

Marta: Not I, signora!... God!

Géméa (catching her breath, misunderstanding): Ah! Marta... Dear,
dear Marta!... Of course!... I understand!... You never take the
credit... But you saved her, that's all that matters!... Please, how
can I thank you?... You, her second mother... You were here, and
you took care of her... And your heart did more than all their science, all their medicine!... And you snatched her from the jaws
of death, my Noémi!... Oh! Bless you, Marta! Bless you!...

Marta: But I...

Géméa: Where is she? I want to see her!

Marta: Only God could perform that miracle... And I called on Him...

Géméa: God?... Whose?

Marta: The one true God... Mine...

Géméa: For a Jew?... You called on your God, for a Jew?

Marta: She... She's not...

Géméa: What? What are you saying? What are you trying to tell me?

Marta: Not any more...

Géméa (*shocked*): My child... Not a Jew?

Marta: She's a Christian now!...

Géméa: My child?

Marta: She was dying! I had to save her!... I...

Géméa: A Christian?... My child?

Marta: And by saving her body, I saved her soul as well!

Géméa (*enraged*): Oh! You... Vile, unclean creature!... You... You foul abomination!... "Saved her" you say?... And who told you that I wouldn't have preferred to see her dead?... Now where is she? Tell me!... I want to see her, this instant!... (*Shrieking*) Where is she?

Marta: Gone!

Géméa: They've stolen my child?... They... (*Menacingly*) You're mad!... Mad, you hear me?... So, my child is a Christian, is she?... My child, my blood... And her blood too... The ancient blood of Israel, proud and unconquered... Her blood will tell... It will raise its voice within her!

Marta: God will silence it.

Géméa: Never!... You can't play with a soul... Or move it from body to body, and expect it to be at peace!

Marta: God will soothe it.

Géméa: No, no!... You can't tear the religion of our ancestors from a heart, and expect it not to leave its roots!

Marta: God will see to it.

Géméa: Oh! Listen to her!... Listen to that statue!... That cold, marble mouth, with all its fine answers...

Marta (*calmly*): Take revenge, if you must...

Géméa: Revenge?... Oh, yes! Yes!... You need have no doubt!... I shall... I will!... But first, tell me where she is! Where have they taken her?... Where is my child?

Marta: I've sworn never to say...

Géméa (*furious*): "Sworn"...? "Sworn"...? She's sworn never to say!... She... What does it matter to me what you've sworn?... My child!... I want my child!... My child, do you understand?... (*Shaking her*) I'll make you tell me!... You're a mother too! You have a son... You will... I'll make you... (*Calling*) Ottavio!... Ottavio!... (*To Marta*) Tell me, or he'll pay! I swear it!... I'll... You'll know what it's like to lose a child, and to lose all hope!... You'll weep for him the way I weep for her!... Because she's dead, you hear me? For me, my child is dead!... And yours will be too! (*Calling*) Ottavio!... Come here!...

Marta: It's no use, he's left... I sent him away... I knew what you would do...

Géméa: Oh! She even robs me of my revenge!... (*To Marta*) Wretch!... Vile, miserable wretch!...

(*She bursts into tears and collapses by the chair, weeping in silence. A moment later, the door, upstage, opens, and Gédéon enters, leaning heavily on his stick, and dragging himself painfully downstage without noticing the two women.*)

Marta (*aside*): Ben-Meïr!...

SCENE 17
Marta, Gédéon, Géméa

Gédéon: Ah... Each step I take is a step closer to the grave... But, weak as I am, at least I can give my child one last embrace. (*Turning to Géméa as she utters a cry*) Géméa!... What is it? What's the matter?

Géméa: The matter?... (*Pointing to Marta*) Her!... That woman!...

Gédéon: Signora Marta?

Géméa: Yes! Look at her!... She's a child-thief!... The house is empty!... Our Noémi is gone...

Gédéon: Gone?

Géméa: Stolen!... Snatched away!... And given to Christians!... (*Pointing to Marta*) Make her talk!... You're a man! Make her tell us where she is!

Gédéon (*staggering*):   Noémi!... My child... Ah! How much more must I bear!

(*He pauses, shaking his head in silent grief.*)

Géméa: Say something!... Do something!... (*Gédéon collapses onto the chair.*) Don't remind me how you dragged me off to Napoli against my will!... I didn't want to leave her, but I had to, you said!... Oh, no! Your uncle couldn't die without me!... "Let's take her," I told you... My precious Noémi!... But no! She would only be in the way!...

Gédéon (*pathetically*):   Géméa...

Géméa: You lusted for his fortune!... Well, now you have it! But where is mine?... My treasure, my life, my soul!... Gone!... Gone!... (*Sobbing*) What? Must I weep alone?... Selfish! Have you no tears, no sorrow?... She's gone, I tell you! Our Noémi is gone!

Gédéon: Géméa...

Géméa: Oh! You wanted your gold!... You yearned for it, dreamed of it!... And it's yours now! You're rich!... You... (*Scornfully*) You shadow of a man! You coward of a father!... But you'll weep tears of blood!... Weep them over and over... And no one will console you in your damnable last days!... Empty... Alone... (*With a long, doleful sigh*) Oh...

(*As she dissolves in tears, Gédéon straightens up as best he can, as if energized by her words. Summoning all his waning strength, he stands up, hobbles over to Marta, and, leaning on his stick, addresses her with all the vigor he can muster.*)

Gédéon (*to Marta*):   You hear?... You hear her curses?... I'm sick, signora! Sick unto death... But with all the strength that's left in this poor body, I entreat you... No, I order you!... Take us to her!... Take us to our child!

———

Marta (*simply*):   I cannot.

Gédéon: Woman begs and weeps! But man commands... Or kills!... (*Menacingly*) Obey! You hear me?

Marta: I did my duty.

Gédéon: I still have the strength to kill you! (*Brandishing his stick at her*) Take care!

Marta: I swore to keep silent. I'll not break my oath.

Gédéon (*suddenly, about to strike her*):   Then die, damn you!

(*Marta, terrified, jumps back, with a scream.*)

Géméa (*holding him back*):   No, no!... For the love of God!... She alone can tell us... If you kill her we'll never know...

Marta (*clutching at her breasts, groaning in pain*):   Ayyy!... My milk... (*Clutching at her throat, staggering*) My heart... My... (*Writhing*) Oh!... The pain... I...

Géméa (*to Gédéon*):   Let me talk to her... Let me beg her, plead with her... There's still hope...

Marta (*clutching feverishly at her head*):   My head... Pins... Needles in my head!... Piercing my brain... My breasts... My whole body...

Géméa (*to Marta, gently*):   Marta!... Dear, dear Marta!... Listen to me! Please!... Forgive me... Forgive us...

Marta (*muttering to herself, raising her eyes heavenward*):   Punishment... My punishment...

Géméa: I beg of you... Where is she?

Marta (weakly):   Ottavio!... Never to see my Ottavio again... My child...

Géméa: Please!... Tell us, Marta!... Tell me!... Think what you've done... To rip a child out of the house of her fathers... To give her the foreigners' god to pray to... Not her poor, weeping mother's... Not to let her understand her... This mother who will die, without even the hope... the sad, sorrowful hope... that one day, at least, she might feel her daughter's bones in the earth beside her!... It's horrible, Marta!... It's a crime!... It's... It's worse! It's a sin... Do you hear?

Marta (clutching at her throat, groaning):   Oh...

Géméa: A sin!... (*Desperate*) I beg of you!... Dear, dear Marta... Sweet Marta... Where is she?... In the name of all that's holy... Where is she?

Marta (collapsing):   Ah...

Géméa (panicked):   What is it?... What's wrong?...

Marta (weakly):   You're avenged... I'm dying...

Géméa: No! Please!... You mustn't... God in heaven!... (*To Gédéon*) Quick! A doctor!... (*Pointing upstage*) Go!... Go!... Find a doctor!

(*Gédéon hobbles out, as quickly as he can.*)

SCENE 18
Marta, Géméa

Marta (close to death, to Géméa):   Pardon me... Please...

Géméa: I do!... I do!... (*Holding her up*) There, there!... See? You're fine!... (*Laying Marta's head on her shoulder*) There!... Dear Marta... Now you can talk... See?... Tell me... Where is she?

Marta (ignoring the question):   Swear you'll never harm my Ottavio...

Géméa: I swear!... (*Growing more and more desperate*) Now please!... In a moment you may be too weak to talk... My Noémi... Where is she?...

Marta (gasping):   Ah...

Géméa: Think what you're doing!... My blood will be on your soul!... Forever!... You're killing me, understand?... God will never forgive you!... Never, do you hear?... Your son's life is in our hands!... (*Looking at her, in terror*) Marta! Do you hear me?... Marta!... Marta!... (*She lets her go and Marta falls to the ground.*) God in heaven!... She's... She's...

(*Gédéon enters, upstage, followed by The Doctor.*)

SCENE 19
Géméa, Gédéon, The Doctor

Géméa: Dottore!... Please! She mustn't die... Don't let her... I'll heap your hands with gold for just one minute of her life!

(*The Doctor feels Marta's pulse.*)

The Doctor (shaking his head):   She's dead...

(*Géméa takes her head in her hands and stands transfixed.*)

Gédéon (pointing to the lifeless Marta):   Those speechless lips, that silent soul... Our eternal damnation...

Géméa (raising her arms to heaven):   God of Abraham, Isaac, and Jacob!... I pledge my soul, to my last dying breath... I pledge my body, to my last drop of blood... I pledge my life, my will, to find my child... I renounce all wealth, and cast from my heart every pleasure, every joy... Perhaps when I have suffered enough... Perhaps then, at last, will you take pity on me, dear God! (*To Gédéon*) Come, Ben-Meïr... Come... We will search every inch of this Italian land... Town by town, house by house, stone by stone, until we find her... And find her we shall!... Come... Come...

(*She takes his arm and leads him slowly off. The Doctor shakes his head in silence as they leave.*)

CURTAIN

Act 1

The scene, upstage, represents a hill, stage right, and a cliff, stage left. Atop the cliff, the façade of a church, vine-covered, with a little garden in front and a practicable door. A stream, part of which can be seen between the hill and the cliff, ostensibly flows behind them. A long staircase leads up the side of the cliff to the church, otherwise inaccessible. Small houses, in perspective, here and there on the hill. Center stage, a village fountain with several water jars standing on its rim. Down right, a small, shabby house, whose façade presents a central door with a window on each side. Down left, two façades: one, that of a little balconied house, and the other, beside it, at the footlights, a tavern, with a sign announcing "Caffè della Polcevera."

At rise, it is early evening. A crowd of villagers occupies the stage, coming and going; some chatting, some humming and singing, others carrying loads and grumbling. A few fishermen sit repairing their nets. A group of monks walk up the staircase, to the church, and disappear inside. Three women, down right, are surrounding Catarina, listening intently to her. Luppo is lying on his back, against the base of the fountain.

SCENE I
Ruccioni, Castara, Frimagusta, Catarina, Luppo, Villagers

Catarina (to The Three Women, pointing to the house, right, as Ruccioni, Castara, and Frimagusta enter, right, passing behind them): Yes... That's where she lives... That hole!... (*As the latter go to the fountain and begin drinking from the jars that the women have laid there*) Believe me! When I say "a witch"... I know what I'm talking about!

The Women: No!...

Catarina: I know one when I see one!... And if you don't think so... What about Muranotti?... You know Muranotti? That handsome

---

devil who would stand and pose whenever you looked at him?...
Well, three days ago she told him he was going to die that very
day... And he died!

The First Woman: He made fun of her, he did!

Catarina: I know... He told her he had a wife and three little ones,
of all things!... But the witch knew he was a bachelor... I can still
see him swaggering off, and laughing... "Me, dead?... Ha ha ha!...
Over my dead body!"

The Second Woman: Oh...

Catarina: And there she is, telling him: "Laugh, corpse!... Laugh!..."
And she was right! Two hours later, he gets himself run through
with a saber!

The Third Woman: They brought his body back...

The First Woman: I saw it...

Catarina: Yes... Well, even before they were anywhere in sight, there
she was, in her doorway, like a hoot-owl, screeching: "The corpse
is coming!"... And she shook all over, and ran inside... (*With a
shudder*) Ah! I love a good fright!... That's why I come here...

(*Bianca enters hurriedly, left. She is heavily veiled and obviously troubled.*)

SCENE 2
Ruccioni, Castara, Frimagusta, Catarina, Luppo, Villagers, Bianca

Bianca (*crossing, to Catarina*):   I beg your pardon... The fortune-
teller... Do you know where I might find her?

Catarina: Fortune-teller?... You mean, the witch?

Bianca: The... Yes...

Catarina (*pointing, right*):   There...

Bianca: Ah...

(*She hesitates for a moment, then approaches the door and knocks. Frigolini opens it and she quickly enters without a word.*)

Frigolini (*taken aback*):   Now who...? No manners, that one, if you
    ask me!...

(*As Ruccioni, Castara, and Frimagusta, having drunk their fill, amble right, toward the house, Frigolini gives Ruccioni a knowing nod and goes back inside, shutting the door.*)

Catarina (*to The Women*):   You see? She must be in there, or Frigolini
    wouldn't have let her go in...

Ruccioni (*to Frimagusta, as the latter stands shaking, looking downstage, over the footlights, ostensibly at a building close by*):   What's the
    matter?

Frimagusta: It's... It's just that every time I see a prison...

Ruccioni (*pointing in the same direction*):   That?... But it's the best one
    in Genova!...

Frimagusta (*shaking his head*):   Still...

(*Loriole enters, right, carrying packs of her wares.*)

SCENE 3
Ruccioni, Castara, Frimagusta, Catarina, Luppo, Villagers, Loriole

Catarina (*noticing her*):   Ah! The peddlar-lady...

Loriole (*putting down her packs, sighing*):   Ah...

Ruccioni (*returning to the well, where his friends are still drinking and chatting, and pointing to Luppo*):   Did you ever see a lazier one?

Catarina (*to Loriole*):   Well now... How goes it today?

Loriole (*replying, with a shrug*):   Today?... Yesterday?...

Ruccioni (*continuing*):   Why I ever took him on I'll never know!

Loriole (*to Catarina, continuing*):   No better... Each day is worse than the one before!

Ruccioni (*continuing*): All he can do is lie on his back... And run when there's trouble!

(*He and his friends sit down around the well and continue chatting, sotto voce.*)

Loriole (*to Catarina and the other Women*):   Believe me, it's not easy to earn a living these days!... If only I knew years ago what I know now! (*Sighing*) Back in Bisagno...

The First Woman: Bisagno?

Loriole: Yes... Long ago, my friend... Seventeen years... (*She sits down on one of her packs, musing.*) And to think, I believed him...

Catarina: Him?...

The Second Woman: A man?

Loriole: A little odd, he was... But, oh! What didn't he promise me?... Oh yes... If only I followed him, I would make a fortune!

The Third Woman (*impressed*):   Oh!

Loriole: And I did...

Catarina: Make a fortune?

Loriole: No!... Follow him... Day after day... And then, one fine day... (*With a snap of the fingers*) Gone!... Disappeared!...

Catarina: Like the rest of them!

The First Woman: Don't they all!

The Second Woman: Of course!

The Third Woman: Tsk tsk tsk!

Loriole (*getting up, to Catarina*):   Are you here to see the fortune-teller?

Catarina: Yes... (*Pointing to The First Woman*) Me and my friend...

Loriole: Me too... But I'll come back... Heart-broken or not, I can wait...

(*She picks up her packs and begins crossing left, singing.*)

Catarina (*to The Women*):   It doesn't sound as if she'll die of sadness, that one!

(*They laugh.*)

Loriole (*to Luppo, who is stretched out in her path*):   Out of the way, you lazy beggar!

(*Luppo, without moving, replies in a mumbled jibberish.*)

Ruccioni (*to Luppo, reprimanding him as Loriole goes around him, continuing left*):   Luppo!

Catarina (*laughing*):   What?... (*To Ruccioni*) What did he say?

Ruccioni: It's his dialect...

Catarina: You understand him?

Ruccioni: He told her to... (*Hesitating*) to... (*Thinking better of it*) No... Never mind...

(*Loriole, at her house, opens the door and disappears inside.*)

Catarina (*to The First Woman*): Aren't your forgetting something?... That present you said you would buy for me when she got here?...

The First Woman (*to the two others*): Come... You two can help me choose...

(*Catarina and The Three Women cross left and exit into Loriole's house.*)

Ruccioni (*pointing to the fortune-teller's house*): That place will make us rich!

Castara: The fortune-teller's?... That shack?

Frimagusta: That hovel?

Ruccioni: Perhaps... But it's worth more than a palace, take my word!

Castara: But she makes her living reading cards!... All over...

Frimagusta (*scornfully*): How much can she be worth?

Castara: Not long ago I saw her in Livorno... They called her "The Magician"... And in Napoli she was "The Sorceress"...

Ruccioni: Luppo even saw her in Palermo!

Frimagusta: And I saw her in Roma!... The Romans called her "The Witch"...

Ruccioni: Sorceress, witch... Magician... What's the difference? Here in Genova she's "The Fortune-Teller"!... So?... If you think that's all she does...

Castara: You mean...?

Ruccioni: I mean, she lends money, my friend... Lots and lots of it!... And not to poor devils like us, believe me!

Frimagusta: And not for a song, I'll bet!

Ruccioni: Exactly!... In less than a year she's lent two hundred thousand piasters... A hundred thousand to the Dorias, fifty thousand to the Capriani brothers, twenty thousand to Cornelius, another thirty to Giustiniani...

Castara: No!

Ruccioni: Yes!... And not a single Jew... (*Pointing right*) Not a single bloodsucking thief has crossed that threshold!... And she hasn't crossed a single one of theirs either!

Frimagusta: What?

Castara: What are you saying?

Ruccioni: Only that, to be able to lend two hundred thousand piasters in ten months... And with no other security than one or two miserable galleys, pledged for three years... Galleys that she's gone and rented out to the king of Spain!... Well, that tells me that she thumbs her nose at money, my friends, and that she must have enough to burn!

Castara (unable to believe his ears): You mean, she's rich?... That... That...

Ruccioni: Well, we'll find out tonight!... We can count on Frigolini... I've made sure of that!...

Frimagusta: Ah...

Ruccioni: So... Here, my friends!... (*The three of them stand up.*) Tonight!... At midnight!...

(*They all shake hands. Castara and Frimagusta exit, right, as Ruccioni
lingers by the fortune-teller's house. Paola and Teresa enter, left, followed,
a moment later, by Ottavio, who hangs back, far left. Pepitta, a little girl,
enters, down right, and goes running up to Paola, happy to see her.*)

SCENE 4
Ruccioni, Paola, Teresa, Ottavio, Pepitta

Pepitta (*to Paola*):   Signora!... Signora!...

Paola: There you are, Pepitta! (*Turning to Teresa*) My little favorite, Teresa...

Ruccioni (*aside*):   Ah!... Signorina Paola Lomellini...

(*He draws back, out of sight.*)

Paola (*to Pepitta, giving her a hug*):   Aren't you going to ask me what
I brought you?

Pepitta: Oh no, signora!... I mustn't!... You're too good to me!

Paola: Well, just for that... (*Giving her a coin*) Here!

Pepitta (*looking at it, wide-eyed*):   Oh!

(*She kisses Paola's hands and goes running off, right.*)

Ottavio: What an angel!

Paola (*turning round, surprised to see him*):   Ottavio!... What on earth...?

Ottavio: I couldn't help watching...

Paola (*joining him, left*):   Have you been following me?

Ottavio: And why not? Aren't we betrothed?... Don't I have the right...?

Paola: But we've spent the last hour, Teresa and I... It's been a whole hour... (*To Teresa*) Did you know? Did you see him?

Teresa (*shaking her head*):   No, signorina...

Ottavio: And I've followed you every step of the way!... Even when you went into that miserable shop and stood arguing over the price of that dainty lace shawl!

Paola: I don't believe it!

Ottavio: Well, it's yours now!

Paola: The shawl?

Ottavio: It's at your palace this very minute... Or it will be...

Paola: You bought it for me?... (*Ottavio gives a good-natured nod.*) You didn't!... What utter folly!

Ottavio: Ah, yes... The last one of my bachelor existence!... You can imagine how they laughed at me... With that lovely delicate thing in these sailor's hands of mine... As if it were so much rigging!

Paola (*with a laugh*):   Oh... (*Turning to Teresa*) Did you ever!...

Ottavio (*continuing*):   "Damnation!" I told them. "Laugh all you

---

47

want!... I'm not one of your soft court signori!... For the last fifteen years a ship has been my home, and a tough old nursemaid—'The Ocean,' by name—has been rocking me to sleep!... Nothing delicate about me, I'm afraid!... The only lace I know are the jagged whitecaps, stretching to the horizon... Like a white fringe under the clear blue sky... And when the tempest blasts, and rips them to shreds, it laughs with its thunderous voice and scatters them over the waves, like so many bits and scraps fleeing in panic..." That's what I told them!

Paola: And in all those years, you never once left your father's ship?

Ottavio: Not once!... He kept me on board day and night... Year in, year out... As if some terrible fate would strike me down if I ever left her... (*Pointing to the church*) That's where he lies!... I can still see him on his deathbed, gasping his last... But he raised up his head, and he looked me square in the eye... "Those wretches killed your mother," he muttered... "Avenge her!"... And then he died!

Paola (*shaking her head*):   Oh...

Ottavio: But his words kept echoing, and they filled me with terror!... And it lasted and lasted, until, one day, when I learned that the danger was past... That they were dead...

Paola: They?... Who?

Ottavio: The man and wife who had sworn they would kill me...

Paola (*as Teresa, listening in rapt attention, crosses herself*):   Good heavens!

Ottavio: At last I could take a peaceful breath! That bloody revenge was lifted from my soul... And thank goodness it was!... To take another life... To murder someone, even in a righteous cause... The mere thought of it terrifies me!

Paola: Ottavio!...

Ottavio: Vengeance or not, I'm no Orestes!... I'll never be a hero!

(*Bianca comes out of the fortune-teller's house, followed by Frigolini.*)

SCENE 5
Ruccioni, still half-hidden, Ottavio, Paola, Teresa, Bianca, Frigolini

Frigolini (*following Bianca out*):   Yes, signora... (*Stopping at the door*)
  I understand... But she may not be returning this evening. And I
  do have other matters to attend to...

Bianca (*at the door*):   Very well... Then I'll come back...

Frigolini: As you wish...

(*He goes back inside. Bianca crosses left, stopping short as she sees Paola.*)

Paola (*surprised to see her*):   Mother!...

Bianca (*taken aback, aside*):   Paola!... (*To Ottavio, aloud*) Good
  evening, count!... (*To Paola, quickly*) Have you found everything
  you wanted?

Paola: Why, yes... (*Wondering what Bianca is doing there*) But...
  What are you—

Bianca (*interrupting her, avoiding her question*):   Lovely things, I'm
  sure!

Paola: Yes... Very... But—

Bianca (*pretending great interest*):   Oh! Tell me!... What?

Paola: Well... For one thing... A beautiful Moorish cape!... You'll
  see...

Bianca: I know it must be a treasure!... (*Not giving her time to speak, to Ottavio*) Count... May I ask you to accompany my daughter to evening prayers?

Paola (to Bianca, quizzically):   Mother...?

Ottavio (to Bianca):   Of course...

Paola (to Bianca):   You aren't coming?

Bianca: I think not... I'm not feeling quite myself...

Paola: But... You're ill, and you didn't tell me?

Bianca: No, no... Not ill... A headache... It's nothing!

Paola (relieved):   Ah... And you came out for a breath of air...

Bianca: Yes... Exactly...

Paola: But you'll come with us, won't you, if your headache goes away?

Bianca: We'll see... Surely you can do without me, I think...

Paola: Could you do without *me?*

Bianca: Oh! Certainly not!

Paola: Then how can I?... What's good for the mother is good for the daughter!

Bianca: But one day, my child, we must... All of us... Sooner or later, life separates us from each other. Why, tomorrow I may lose you!

Paola: Never! Don't even think such a horrible thing!

Bianca: But you're getting married! Your new family...

Paola: My new family and my own will be one and the same... My heart will know no difference! (*Pointing to Ottavio*) Ottavio is my witness... I belong to the husband that my mother chose for me, and to the mother that God gave me!

Bianca (*touched*): My dear...

Paola (*continuing*): I can lay my soul before you, simple and sincere... (*To Ottavio*) Had I been free to choose, Ottavio... Had I had before me all the most noble and most worthy suitors, you would have been my choice!... All the proudest, all the grandest... No other has ever shared my heart, nor ever will. My first memory is of you. My last thought will be yours...

Ottavio: Paola...

Paola: Ah, Ottavio... The moment I laid eyes on you, it was as if I knew you... As if your image had been graven on my soul... You barely smiled, and already I was yours! You scarcely spoke, and I was ready to do your bidding!

Ottavio: Dearest...

Paola: But in spite of all my love... All the passion that blinds my poor, defenseless heart... In spite of it all, Ottavio, were you to come to me tomorrow, and say: "You must choose between your mother and me!..." (*Sighing*) Ah!... It would kill me, perhaps, but I would have to choose my mother!

Bianca (*to Ottavio*): Forgive her, count! (*Good-naturedly*) She's spoiled beyond belief!

Paola: And whose fault is that? (*To Bianca*) Would you have listened if I had tried to scold you?... My slightest wish, my merest whim... And who was always there to grant it? Who would always tell me:

"Ask for it, and it's yours!"...? Who would try to make my every dream come true?... (*Sighing, to Ottavio*) Ah!... Not only a mother, Ottavio, but a friend... And each one was there to soften the other's anger... When the mother would scold, the friend would smile... When the friend was cross, the mother would hug and kiss!... (*Shaking her head*) Both of them, too good... (*To Bianca*) Yes... Too good!... You gave me everything you had in life... Everything but your troubles... Everything you had in your heart, but your tears.

Ottavio: Ah, Paola! I love you all the more...

Bianca (*to Ottavio*): Yes... Love her, count!... Her heart will never fail you... (*To Paola*) I know what makes it beat... I know those tender thoughts... (*To Ottavio, as Paola is about to object*) Ask her, count... Ask her why she loves to pass through these narrow streets, and to come to this crowded, teeming square... (*Before he can comply*) No, I'll tell you... It's because it was here, one day, when she was visiting the poor, that she first met her Count Ottavio...

Paola: Mother...

Bianca (*continuing*): And that's why she comes here, every night, for evening prayers... (*Pointing*) Trudging up to that church... Because she knows that your father, the admiral, Count d'Oriani, is resting in peace beneath the high altar... When she prays to God she thinks of the father, and when she prays for the father she dreams of the son... (*To Paola*) Am I wrong?

Paola: Please... If you must... (*Eager to change the subject*) You should be scolding him instead!... Do you know what that spendthrift did?... Can you imagine?... He went and bought me the most beautiful lace shawl... In our palace this very minute!... And whenever I put it on, I'll feel two thousand crowns pressing down on my shoulders!

Ottavio: Just the first gift of many, for my bride-to-be...

Paola: But so soon?... Even before my father arrives? Before he gives his blessing?... (*To Bianca*) He's so sure of our marriage!... It can only bring bad luck!

Bianca (aside): Her father... Ah me!

Ottavio (to Paola, jovially): Superstitious!

Paola (to Ottavio, likewise): Wait and see!

Bianca: You're mad, both of you...

Paola (to Bianca): Come... It's time we went home...

(*She takes Bianca's arm and all three begin to move off, right.*)

Ruccioni (stepping out of the shadows, to Ottavio): A word with you, my noble friend...

Ottavio (waving him off): Later...

Ruccioni: It's a matter that concerns you...

Ottavio: All the more reason...

Bianca (to Ottavio, with a note of sarcasm): See what the gentleman has to say... We'll not go far...

(*She and Paola exit, right.*)

SCENE 6
Ottavio, Ruccioni

Ottavio: You?... Whoever you are!... So, we meet again...

Ruccioni: True... Your memory is good, count!... Three times in ten years... And each time, to warn you... The first, of a danger...

Ottavio: I avoided it.

Ruccioni: The second, of a treason...

Ottavio: I foiled it.

Ruccioni: And now, the third time, to warn you of a trap...

Ottavio: Who are you?

Ruccioni (ignoring the question, continuing): Salviati, your father, began as a simple sailor. But, thanks to his genius and his daring, by the time he died he was Count d'Oriani... An admiral and a millionaire!...

Ottavio: And...?

Ruccioni: And that makes you one of the richest nobles in Genova... Which means that, when you take yourself a wife, she must be beautiful... which Paola Lomellini is!... and rich... which she is not!

Ottavio: What?

Ruccioni: At least, no longer!

Ottavio: What are you saying?

Ruccioni: Simply that the Lomellini fortune, all their vast wealth, is the island of Taberca... The "Coral Isle," as the fishermen call it... And it brings them in a good three hundred thousand piasters a year, in round figures... Give or take...

Ottavio (growing impatient): And...?

Ruccioni: Now, the island of Taberca seems to have fallen to the Turks... Of course, no one has told you!... But a friend of mine has just come from there... The island was bombarded and taken by the bey of Tunis... The Lomellinis are ruined! Their fortune... Up in smoke!... Marry their daughter, and you fall into their trap... Poor innocent victim...

Ottavio: Why should I believe you?

Ruccioni: It's none of my business, but I thought you should know... Call it a good deed! (*Aside*) To balance all my bad ones!

Ottavio: Wasn't it you that her father had expelled from the shipyards two years ago?

Ruccioni: Yes... But for no good reason... I wanted to reform and work for an honest living.

Ottavio: No doubt... And now you want to avenge the disgrace!... Well, victim for victim, I'll not be yours, my friend!... I don't believe you!

Ruccioni: As you wish...

(*He withdraws, upstage.*)

Ottavio (*aside*): Ruined...? Poor child... Well, what does it matter? My fortune is more than enough for us all.

(*He exits, right.*)

SCENE 7
Ruccioni, alone

Ruccioni: Bah!... At that age all they think about is marriage... And Paola Lomellini, after all... As much as I hate her father, I can't help loving her!... (*Pointing right*) For his sake, at least... Handsome young devil!... (*Musing*) And Marta's son!... Ah! If she only knew... (*Shrugging his shoulders*) Perhaps she does... (*Looking heav-*

enward) And how happy she must be!... Little does he dream that I used to hold him on my lap!... Well, I don't have to tell him my name to watch over him... It's not much to be proud of... Perhaps if I were an admiral... Or even a doge...

(*He gives a whistle. A moment later Frigolini comes running out of the fortune-teller's house.*)

SCENE 8
Ruccioni, Frigolini

Frigolini (*to Ruccioni*):   Not tonight!... It's impossible...

Ruccioni: What?... (*Furious*) What do you take us for, you...

Frigolini: My plan won't work!...

Ruccioni: You... What kind of game...

Frigolini: It was perfect!... Géméa told me to follow a certain young lady, and find out who she was... (*Pointing toward the stream*) Someone she saw last week, in a little boat... A kind of gondola...

Ruccioni: So?

Frigolini: You can guess what my plan was!... I was going to go tell her parents that the old hag was trying to get their daughter in trouble!... Damn sure they would have had her locked up, good and proper!... (*Pointing out over the footlights toward the supposed prison*) Rich people like that can just snap their fingers and have someone put away!...

Ruccioni (*losing patience*):   Go on! Go on!...

Frigolini: Anyway, while they were dragging her off, you and the others would come and break down the door...

Ruccioni: Well?

Frigolini: Well, the problem was, I didn't know enough about her!...
You know how many young blond women I found?... Eighteen
or nineteen...?

Ruccioni (misunderstanding):   So? That's not very many...

Frigolini: What?... (*Realizing his confusion*) No, no... Years old!...
Eighteen or nineteen years old, my friend!... I must have found a
couple hundred!... There's a damn swarm of them in this city!...
And in a gondola... With a coral shield on the stern... Is that
enough to go on, I ask you?

Ruccioni (pricking up his ears):   A coral shield, you say?... On the
stern?

Frigolini: Yes... There must be dozens!

Ruccioni: Idiot!... That's Paola Lomellini, you dolt!... She must have
got it from the fishermen of Taberca...

Frigolini: Ah... Well, in that case... Quick! Where does she live?

Ruccioni: Next to the Dorias... A palace... All white...

Frigolini: With big marble pillars?

Ruccioni: Exactly!

Frigolini: Then I'm on my way!... (*He begins running off, right, then
stops suddenly and returns.*) Tonight, then?... At midnight?

Ruccioni: Yes!... (*Tugging on Frigolini's ear.*) If your brain is still
working!

Frigolini: And I'll get my share?

Ruccioni: Of course!

Frigolini: The same as all the rest of you?

Ruccioni (impatiently): Yes! Yes!... Now go!...

Frigolini (dashing off, right, to himself): Gold!... Gold!... I'll be rich!...

(*As he exits, The Villagers come crowding back, talking amongst themselves and pointing their fingers at the fortune-teller's house. At the same time, Loriole comes out of her house, followed by The Three Women, carrying various bundles.*)

SCENE 9
Ruccioni, Loriole, Catarina, The Three Women, Villagers

Loriole (crossing right, to Catarina and The Three Women): I'm happy that you found what you wanted, my friends...

The First Woman: Yes... And now... (*Going to the fortune-teller's house, timidly, and about to knock*) Oh!... (*Moving back*) I don't dare!

Loriole: Come!... I'll go too!

The Second Woman: So will I!

The Third Woman: Me too...

(*They approach the door and Loriole gives several determined knocks.*)

Ruccioni (aside): She'd board a privateer without blinking, that one!

Loriole: No answer... Perhaps she's not at home... (*To a burly Villager*) You... Benedetto!... Come here!... (*Going over to Luppo, who is still lying by the fountain, nudging him with her toe*) And you!... Come! Be useful...

(*Luppo reluctantly gets up, grumbling incomprehensibly, and follows her and The Villager over to a window of the house.*)

Loriole (*to Luppo*):   Here... Give him a boost... He'll look in the window...

(*The Villager is about to climb up on Luppo's shoulders.*)

Ruccioni (*aside*):   A good chance to get the lay of the land!... (*Waving The Villager aside*) No, no... Let me...

(*He climbs up on the still grumbling Luppo's shoulders and peers inside.*)

Catarina (*to Ruccioni*):   Well? What do you see?... Is she in there?

Ruccioni (*getting down, as Luppo goes back to the fountain and resumes his position*):   It's hard to say... (*In a mock-mysterious tone*) Ah yes!... I saw something!... But human?... Who can tell? (*As Catarina and The Women shudder*) It was crouching in a corner... In the dark... And it had a distinctly sinister look about it!

Catarina: Oh...

The First Woman (*as the other two gasp*):   Good heavens!

Loriole (*to Catarina*):   Don't listen to him!... He's joking!

Ruccioni (*laughing*):   No matter! She can still steal your money!

Catarina (*to Ruccioni*):   Sweet Jesus, signore! Don't say such a thing!

The First Woman (*to Ruccioni*):   She'll curse you!

Ruccioni (*laughing*):   No doubt!

Catarina: Besides, she told my fortune and it didn't cost me a thing!

Loriole: Oh?

Catarina: She told me I would be rich some day!

Ruccioni: Yes... I can see your rags are looking better and better!

Catarina (reproaching him, angrily): So? I'm poor enough for two and not wealthy enough for one! That doesn't mean it will never come true!

Loriole (pulling her away): Come, come!... Our fearless captain likes to tease... And all the better when he finds a defenseless woman to make fun of!

(*Several of The Villagers, obviously impatient, have begun pointing at the fortune-teller's house and muttering amongst themselves.*)

Ruccioni (to Loriole): Not at all, lovely lady... (*With a wide gesture*) It's just that, if all of you want your silly fortunes told... So many of you at once... Perhaps she has other things to do! Put yourself in her place...

(*As The Villagers shake their fists and become more vociferous, with shouts of "Sorceress!... Gypsy!... She-devil!... Old hag!..." and the like, some even throwing stones at her house, Géméa appears at her door, so absorbed in her thoughts that she seems unaware of her antagonists. Ruccioni withdraws to the fringes of the crowd.*)

SCENE 10
Géméa, Ruccioni, Loriole, Catarina, The Three Women, Villagers

Géméa (to herself): Why must she be so hard to find, this young beauty?... The image of Gédéon, I swear...

Catarina (to the others): I'm going to ask her... I must... (*Approaching Géméa*) Now that my daughter has been found...

Géméa (overhearing, turning to her, quickly):   Found?... A daughter?...
Where? When...?

Catarina (aside):   God! Those eyes...

Géméa: Where...? Where is she?

Catarina: My Pepitta, signora...

Géméa: Your...

Catarina: Her father had taken her from me... But he's dead. And
now I have her back.

Géméa (hanging her head):   Ah...

Catarina: But I'm worried about the future... Mine... Hers... What
can you tell me?

Géméa (muttering to herself):   Her child... Her daughter...

Catarina: You read palms too, don't you?... Not only cards... (*Holding out her palm*) Here... Please!... Tell me what you see...

(*Géméa takes her hand, looks at it, sighing.*)

Géméa: I see...

Loriole (to the others):   Oh!... She's reading it!... She's going to tell
her something...

(*The Villagers look on, expectantly.*)

Géméa (to Catarina):   I see... You have a daughter... (*The Villagers
"ooh" and "aah" in admiration.*) You will always be happy... So it is
written!

Catarina (*incredulously*):   Me?... Happy?

Géméa: The tree without fruit lives a cursèd existence!

Catarina (*still unable to believe her ears*):   Me?

Géméa (*turning to leave, right*):   Never let her out of your sight, signora!... Or disaster... (*Muttering to herself*) Disaster...

Loriole (*stopping her*):   Wait!... It's my turn!... (*Holding out a coin*) Look! I'll pay!

(*Géméa gives her a look of utter scorn. Loriole pulls back, frightened.*)

Géméa (*aside, as The Women gesture and chatter amongst themselves*): Why should I give up now?... I did see her once... Three days after the disaster...

Loriole: Heaven help me! Those eyes...

Géméa (*continuing, aside*):   My Noémi... Yes, I saw her in a carriage... And a woman, with a veil... Clutching her to her breast!...

Loriole (*to Catarina and The Women*):   Did you see that look she gave me?

Géméa (*continuing, aside*):   Oh! That vile beast!... (*As if reliving the scene*) I threw myself in front of the horses, and... I clung to the door, and... I tugged, and pulled it open... Gasping and scratching...

Loriole (*continuing*):   I swear it was a curse!

Géméa (*continuing, aside*):   Scratching her vile, unholy flesh!... But she pulled the door tight, and... I fell to the ground...

Catarina and *The Women* (*crossing themselves, to Loriole*):   No!

Géméa (*continuing, aside*):   The wheels ran over me, and the carriage disappeared!... And my poor Noémi... My child... Gone... Gone...

(*She goes over and sits down in front of her house.*)

Loriole (*to The Women*):   You can talk to her if you like!... Not me, thank you!

Géméa (*aside*):   No! It's too soon to give up!... With my gold, my magic...

The First Woman (*to The Second Woman*):   You!...

The Second Woman: Oh no!... (*To The Third Woman*) You!...

Géméa (*continuing, aside, with a look of scorn at the crowd*):   With their greed, their superstition, I can turn the world upside down to find her!... (*With determination, to herself, as The Women continue to demur*) So! Dry your tears, poor wretch!... Seventeen years... But the secret shall be mine!

The Third Woman (*to The First Woman*):   You!... You're the one who wanted to...

Géméa (*continuing, to herself*):   It shall be! I swear... (*Aloud, as if in a sudden frenzy, to The Women*) Ahhh!... The powers... The powers...

The Women (*taken aback*):   Oh!...

Géméa (*shouting*):   They wish to be heard!... (*Beckoning*) Come!... Come!... I must speak!... The stars...

Loriole (*to The Women*):   What's got into her?

Géméa: The powers... My magic...

Catarina: Good God!

Géméa: Life and death... Come!... Come!... (*She throws off her cape and spreads it on the ground.*) The cards!... Yes! The cards!... (*She crouches and begins dealing the cards, chanting, eerily.*)

Beneath the moon!
Come bale! Come boon!
Babies flying!
Mothers crying!...

(*Beckoning*) Come!... Come!... The cards are going to speak!... The cards... The powers... Come!...

(*As The Women draw near, timidly, Frigolini enters, right.*)

Frigolini (*to Géméa, in a whisper*): I've found her!

Géméa: Ah...? (*Excitedly*) And...?

Frigolini (*continuing*): Her name is Paola Lomellini... She lives in a palace, next to the Dorias...

Géméa: So!

Frigolini (*continuing*): All white... With marble pillars...

(*Géméa hurriedly picks up the cards and throws on her cape.*)

Loriole (*to Géméa*): What are you doing?

Géméa: Later!

Catarina: But... The powers...

Géméa: Tomorrow!

The First Woman: The stars...

Géméa: Not now!... Not now!...

(*As they continue to object, she goes running off, right.*)

Loriole: Oh! Did you ever...

The First Woman: She's making fun...

Catarina: She's making fools of us...

(*As Frigolini approaches Ruccioni, upstage, Catarina and The Three Women, along with the other Villagers, go chasing after Géméa with shouts of "Old witch!... Damned sorceress!..." and such. Loriole, far right, watches them go.*)

Frigolini (*to Ruccioni*):   It's done!... The people in the palace know... You can bet she'll be arrested!

Ruccioni: Ah!

Frigolini: And lucky if they don't stone her first!...

Ruccioni: Good!... (*Noticing Loriole*) Shhh!... (*Indicating her with a nod, whispering*) Over there... You'd better leave...

Frigolini (*whispering*):   Midnight, signore...

(*He exits, left. Ruccioni crosses to the staircase leading up the cliff, and sits down. Loriole peers at him from a distance, more and more intently.*)

SCENE II
Loriole, Ruccioni

Loriole (*aside*):   No... No doubt about it!... I've seen that scoundrelly face before!... But where?... (*Searching her memory*) I... I wonder... (*Drawing a little closer*) No!... Is it?... Could it be...? Oh! I don't believe... (*Drawing closer, still aside*) Yes! It... It could be, God help me!... At least, I think... Well, Let's find out... (*Approaching him, aloud, very formally*) God save you, noble stranger!

Ruccioni (*getting up*):   From what, lovely lady?

Loriole: Ill fortune, of course...

Ruccioni: What other kind is there? That's the only kind I know!... (*Suggestively*) Unless you would like to change it...

Loriole: Me?

Ruccioni: And why not?

Loriole: Oh? Do you wear your heart on your sleeve, signore?

Ruccioni (*holding out his arm*):   Here! See for yourself...

Loriole (*taking it*):   How can I refuse?

Ruccioni (*aside*):   I said she could board a privateer without blinking!

Loriole (*aside*):   Him...? Maybe... (*Aloud*) Signore... If you please... I have a favor to ask of you...

Ruccioni: Ask away, lovely lady!... Only, start at the end. My time is valuable, and every minute counts!

Loriole: Indeed!... The fact is, I'm to be a godmother...

Ruccioni: And... Let me guess!... You want me as the godfather!

Loriole: Precisely!

Ruccioni: Well, it wouldn't be the first time!... Years ago, in Bisagno...

Loriole: I knew it!... It *is* you!... You *are*...

Ruccioni: I am?... Of course I am!... (*Quizzically*) "Are" what...? And... Who...?

Loriole: Loriole!... Mademoiselle Loriole!...

Ruccioni (*agog*): You?... Loriole?... You mean... (*Scrutinizing her*) Good God in heaven! You're right!... (*Delighted*) You are!...

Loriole (*echoing him*): I am?... Of course I am!...

Ruccioni: By all the saints... (*He throws his arms around her and gives her a huge hug.*) You!... Loriole!... (*Looking her up and down*) I must say, the years have been good to you!

Loriole: You scoundrel!... Where have you been?... Seventeen years!... I've been looking for you, high and low!

Ruccioni: And in between, I'll bet!...

Loriole (*jovially*): Hold your tongue!

Ruccioni: With plenty of stops along the way!... Just to compare!...

Loriole (*pretending to be shocked, pulling away*): Oh!... And what have you been doing all this time, may I ask?

Ruccioni: Me?... A little good, a little bad... And lots of nothing at all!... And you?

Loriole: Me?... (*With a little good-natured affectation*) Why... I'm a purveyor of household wares, signore.

Ruccioni: Aha... A peddlar...

Loriole: Well... You might say... But I have the finest clientele in Genova!

Ruccioni: Brava!... Brava!... (*Gently sarcastic*) When you're not too busy being a godmother, that is!...

Loriole: When I... Yes! Precisely!... (*Changing the subject*) By the way... That godchild of yours... That baby... Remember?

Ruccioni: In Bisagno?

Loriole: Yes... What ever became of her?

Ruccioni: Who knows?

Loriole: A fine godfather you turned out to be!

Ruccioni: Whose fault...? I never heard another word... At least, I'm sure she's not a baby any more!

Loriole: Chances are... And her parents?

Ruccioni: They tell me the father died... And the mother disappeared...

Loriole: And you never saw her again?

Ruccioni: Again? Who...?

Loriole: Géméa... Wasn't that her name?

Ruccioni: No... That is, yes, that was her name... But no, I never saw her... Not again, not before... I wouldn't know her if I did!

Loriole: Ah...

Ruccioni (changing the subject): You know, she may even be married by now...

Loriole: Her mother?

Ruccioni: No, no! The child...

Loriole: Bah! (*Jovially*) Who would do a foolish thing like that?

Ruccioni (taking her arm, looking at her ring finger): Not you, I see...

Loriole (taking his, likewise): Nor you...

(*They stand for a moment, hand in hand, exchanging embarrassed smiles, not knowing what to say.*)

Ruccioni (finally): No... I'm still looking...

Loriole: For a dowry of a thousand crowns?

Ruccioni: Not even... For just the right woman... A real one...

Loriole: But a dowry wouldn't hurt!

Ruccioni: Well...

Loriole: Keep looking, my friend!...

Ruccioni (as she turns, about to leave): Could you use a piaster or two?

Loriole (proudly): Me?... Ha ha!... With the best clientele in Genova?

Ruccioni (holding her back): Too bad... Because tomorrow... You never know... The tide may go out and forget to come in!... Can I give you some advice?

Loriole: If I don't have to pay for it...

Ruccioni (*seriously*):   If something wakes you up in the middle of the night, don't go looking out the window!

Loriole: Oh?... Why on earth...?

Ruccioni: Because I say so... (*Pointing to her house*) And now, are you going to invite me to supper?

Loriole: If you promise to tell me everything!

Ruccioni (*shaking his head*):   Tsk tsk tsk!... Just remember, I have to be out by midnight!

Loriole: Oh, you will... You will...

(*He offers her his arm and they cross left, together. As they exit into her house, Ottavio arrives, right, followed by Géméa, her hands bound, led by Two Guards.*)

SCENE 12
Géméa, Ottavio, The Two Guards

The First Guard (*giving Géméa a shove*):   We'll make you talk, believe me!

Ottavio (*reproaching him*):   Please!... No violence, I said...

The Second Guard: Damned thief!...

The First Guard: To prison with her...

Géméa (*pointing, as best she can, to her house*):   Go!... Look inside my house... You'll see it's not the house of a thief, signori...

Ottavio (*to Géméa*):   What were you doing in the palace?

Géméa (ignoring his question):   Poor, miserable hovel... (*To The Guards*) You have my keys... Go... Look...

Ottavio (insisting):   Am I going to have to force you?

Géméa: Oh, you can, of course!... You're strong... And the law is on your side...

Ottavio (impatiently):   What were you doing there?

Géméa (continuing her evasive reply):   All I can do is bow my head and pray... Pray, signore... And swear to you that I am not a thief... That I wished no one any harm... As God is my witness...

Ottavio: Once again... (*Sternly*) What were you doing in the palace?

Géméa: I saw a young lady on the balcony... I wanted to see what she looked like, and so I went in...

Ottavio: Do you know her?

Géméa: Not at all...

Ottavio: What did you want with her?

Géméa: Nothing...

Ottavio: You realize what will happen if you refuse to speak?

Géméa: My fate is in your hands...

Ottavio: Where are you from?

Géméa: From everywhere, signore... Milano, Livorno, Napoli, Firenze... I've been to them all, and more... Looking... Searching...

Ottavio (aside): Strange old hag!... (*Aloud*) And I suppose it was that search that brought you to Genova, to the Lomellinis' palace!... And that made you climb the double fence, and risk being stoned, or beaten to death?... What kind of search...?

Géméa: No need to say... God knows, and that's enough... (*Bitterly*) They tell me I'm mad!... Well, perhaps I am... Mad enough to be thrown into a dungeon in Firenze... Ten years ago, signore... Mad enough for them to think I was a spy... And mad enough to keep searching the minute they set me free...

Ottavio: Signora...

Géméa: And now, again... Shackled like a common thief!... Yes... Mad, I'm sure... Because nothing will stop me...

Ottavio: Are you looking for someone?

Géméa: No...

Ottavio: Family?

Géméa: I have none.

Ottavio: Your husband?

Géméa: He's dead.

Ottavio: A child, perhaps?

Géméa (with a sarcastic sneer): Me?... This miserable wreck of a woman?... A mother?... Ha!... (*As she begins to weep*) Let my tears be your answer...

Ottavio: For the last time, will you tell me... (*As she turns aside*) No?... (*To The Guards, pointing out over the footlights*) Take her to the prison!

Géméa (*falling to her knees before him*):   No!... Mercy, signore!... Mercy!... Not the prison! Please!... I beg you... My poor husband died there... Out of his mind...

Ottavio: Talk! You still have time...

Géméa (*getting up, to The Guards*):   Then take me... I'm ready...

(*As they begin to comply, Ottavio interrupts them.*)

Ottavio (*to The Guards*):   No... No need... (*Waving them off*) You may go!

(*They exit, right.*)

Ottavio (*freeing Géméa's hands, aside*):   As stubborn as she is mad, poor creature!... (*To Géméa*) You're free, signora... (*Pointing to her house*) Free to go home...

Géméa: Ah!... Bless you!... Bless you, young man!... (*Kissing his hands*) I'm free... And there's still hope, you hear?... God listens to the prayers of the humblest souls! You see?... He does! He does!... And I'll pray for you... (*Ottavio gestures to calm her enthusiasm.*) I will!... As if you were my son... My very own...

Ottavio: Thank you... But...

Géméa: Where are you from?

Ottavio: Close by... From the valley... La Polcevera...

Géméa (*with a note of scorn*):   Oh?... One of them?... One of those... those... (*Changing her tone*) No matter!... I'll never forget what you have done!

Ottavio: I was born in Bisagno...

Géméa (taken aback): Bisagno!... In Bisagno, you say?... And your name?... What's your name?

Ottavio: Ottavio Salviati... Count d'Oriani...

Géméa (agape, almost speechless): Sal... Salviati... Then you are... Marta Salviati was...

Ottavio: My mother, signora...

Géméa (exclaiming): You!... You!... *(Aside)* Marta's son!... *(Aloud)* God in heaven!

Ottavio (curious): Did you know her?

Géméa: Know her?... Did I know know her? That child-thief?

Ottavio: That... *(Aghast)* Then you... You're Géméa!... You...

Géméa: So!... You know your mother's crime, I see!... Her foul, vicious crime...

Ottavio: You!... *(Crossing himself)* By all that's holy... You!... The woman who draped our house in mourning!... *(Beside himself)* Her!... That...

Géméa: Yes, her!... And as desperate now as she was that day!... As wild and as fierce!... And she'll never give up... No peace in her soul... No hope in her heart...

Ottavio (pointing up right, to the church, menacingly): Beware, signora!... My father's bones lie buried in that church! The father who cursed you till his dying day...

Géméa: "Beware," you tell me?... I should beware?... I, who have my own vengeance to perform?... Ah, no!... It's you!... You, who should beware, my friend!... I'll follow you, haunt your every step!... Your every joy... Your happiness... Your love!

Ottavio: Yes! Follow me you shall!... In chains!... To the dungeon... To the gallows!

Géméa: You think so, do you?... And what will you say to condemn me? Tell me... That your mother repaid my kindnesses with the vilest of treachery?... That she stole my child, my babe, my only treasure?... That my husband died of grief?... And that I, for seventeen years, have wept my bitter tears alone?... That my grief and my despair will surely kill me?... Is that what you will say?... Come, tell me! I want to hear it!... From your very own lips...

Ottavio: I'm warning you...

Géméa (*holding out the cords with which she had been bound*):   Here!... Bind me!... Do your duty! Beat me!... No matter... Nothing will stop me from cursing you, you hear?... Nothing will stop me from calling down your doom upon you!... You!... You!... Marta's son!... (*Holding out her hands*) Here!... (*In a frenzy*) Bind my hands, I tell you!

Ottavio: Leave!... Before I forget that you're mad!... Before you regret your folly...

Géméa (*turning to leave*):   Oh! We shall meet again... (*Scornfully*) Count d'Oriani!

Ottavio: So much the worse for you if we do!

Géméa: I swear it!... We shall!...

(*The church bells begin to ring. Ottavio and Géméa fall silent as they see Paola entering, up right, borne in a sedan-chair by Two Porters.*)

Ottavio, Géméa, Paola, The Two Porters

Paola (*to The Porters*):   Please!... This is far enough... The climb is too steep...

The First Porter: But for you, signorina...

Paola: No, no... The count will help me...

(*She steps down and The Two Porters exit, up right.*)

Géméa (*aside*):   Paola Lomellini!

Ottavio (*to Paola*):   Please forgive me... I've kept you waiting...

Géméa (*staring at her, aside*):   My God!... Gédéon's eyes!... Gédéon's mouth!...

Ottavio (*to Paola*):   Come... Take my arm...

Géméa (*aside*):   And just the age my Noémi would be!

Paola (*recoiling as she catches sight of Géméa*):   Her!... Again!... (*To Ottavio, pointing*) That woman...

Ottavio: Come... Come...

Paola (*aside*):   Looking at me... Staring... (*To Ottavio*) But who is she? Do you know her?

Ottavio: Her name is Géméa...

Paola: A foreigner?

Ottavio: A Jewess...

Paola (horrified):   A Jewess?...

Géméa (with a dejected sigh, aside):   Ah... My name... Her race...

Paola (crossing herself):   Good heavens!

Géméa (continuing, aside):   No echo in her soul... No pity in her
heart... (*Sobbing*) My Noémi would have known... Somehow...
Somehow... God would have shown her...

Paola (to Ottavio):   But why is she weeping?

Géméa (aside):   My Noémi!... My treasure!... Where are you, my
child?... If you lie in the grave, will my tears not wake you?

Ottavio (to Paola, ignoring her question):   Come... The church bells
are ringing...

Géméa (continuing, aside):   And if you still live, will they not bring
you to me?

(*She collapses onto the steps of her house, and sits weeping.*)

Paola (moved):   Poor thing!... It breaks my heart to see her...

Ottavio (to Paola, insisting):   Please!... The prayers are beginning...

Paola: Oh! How ashamed I feel!... Jewess or not... The poor soul
seems to be suffering so... (*Offering Géméa her purse*) Here, signora... Take this...

Géméa (with a gesture):   No!... Keep your gold...

Ottavio (to Paola):   Come...

Géméa (aside):   Your filthy gold!...

Paola (*to Géméa*):   Are you so proud?

Géméa (*with a fierce look*):   And why should I not be?... Tell me!...
Have I not the right...?

Paola (*drawing back*):   Oh!... Those eyes!... That frightful scowl!...
(*To Ottavio*) Come, Ottavio... Quickly!...

Ottavio (*aside*):   Would she wreak her vengeance on her as well?

Paola (*pulling him up left, toward the staircase leading up the
cliff*):   Come!... Please!...

(*She and Ottavio begin climbing the stairs.*)

Géméa (*to herself, watching them leave*):   Frightful scowl?... Well, so
be it!... At least, no more tears!... No... (*Drying her eyes*) No more
tears, Géméa!... It's another's turn to shed them now!... To weep
and mourn... (*Getting up*) And weep he shall!... Ah yes! He shall!...
Woe unto you, Ottavio, son of Marta!... Ottavio Salviati!... Woe
unto you, count!... Woe!... Woe!... (*With utter contempt*) Count
d'Oriani!...

(*She exits to her house as Ottavio and Paola reach the church door and
disappear inside. As the bells stop ringing, Luppo, still lying against the
fountain, awakens. He stands up, stretches, scratches his head, and, mumbling to himself, exits, left.*)

CURTAIN

Act 2

A poorly furnished room in Géméa's house. Upstage center, the door leading to the outside, flanked by two windows, seen from the other side in Act ɪ. Down right, a door leading off to other rooms. In the corner, up right, a small table with a dimly lighted lamp, providing the only faint light in the room. Down right, a large table covered with a shabby cloth on which are spread cards of varying sizes. In the middle of it, a skull and an hourglass. On a corner of the table, an inkwell, quill, and paper. Two chairs, at the table, one facing the foot-lights, and the other facing stage left. Along the left wall, several armoires and trunks. Other appropriate furnishings—astrological charts, mystical paraphernalia, etc.—*ad libitum*.

At rise, it is night. Géméa is seated at the large table, her head in her hands, deep in thought.

SCENE I
Géméa, Ruccioni, Castara, Frimagusta, Frigolini

Géméa (*to herself*):   Yes!... Revenge!... Oh yes... Yes, yes... (*Tapping her forehead*) In here... Every detail... (*As she continues reflecting, the windows and upstage door begin to open slowly.*) Only... How?... Who...?

(*Castara and Frimagusta, masked, come climbing quietly through the windows. Ruccioni and Frigolini, also masked, come in the door, all unseen by Géméa, whose back is turned.*)

Géméa (*still deep in thought*):   Someone to carry it out for me... (*As the four stop in their tracks, surprised to see her*) Someone...

Ruccioni (*to Frigolini in a whisper*):   She's here!... (*Angrily*) I thought you said...

Géméa (continuing):   Someone I can trust...

Frigolini (to Ruccioni, whispering):   I don't understand... I was sure...

(*Ruccioni gives him a gesture of disgust.*)

Ruccioni (aloud, to Géméa):   Your keys, signora!

Géméa (roused, turning round):   What?... (*Getting up*) Who...?

Ruccioni (demanding):   Your keys! And be quick!... Not another word...

(*Frimagusta and Castara have begun rummaging about the table, throwing the cards onto the floor in disarray.*

Géméa: My keys, you say?... (*Sardonically*) Why, of course, my masked friend...

(*She hands him several keys, which he distributes among the others, who begin eagerly opening all her armoires and trunks.*)

Castara (opening an armoire):   Empty!

Frimagusta (opening a trunk, looking inside):   Nothing but rags!

Castara: Nothing!... Not a thing!...

Géméa (laughing):   You see? The old witch has been expecting you!... Poor fools!... If it's gold you're after... (*Throwing a handful of coins on the floor.*) Here!... I'm happy to oblige!

Frimagusta: Oh...

Castara: Look!...

(*As Castara, Frimagusta, and Frigolini grovel about for the gold, Géméa stands watching them intently.*)

Géméa: Interesting...

Ruccioni: And why, may I ask?

Géméa: You are not like your friends, signore...

Ruccioni: Oh?

Géméa: If so little makes them happy, they cannot want much!... But you, on the other hand...

Ruccioni: Me...?

Géméa: Yes... You want much more!... And unless I much mistake, you can earn it!... (*Suggestively*) Perhaps I can help you...

Ruccioni: You?

Géméa: Would you like to work for me?

Ruccioni: Would I... (*With a laugh*) Would you trust me?

Géméa (*seizing his mask and ripping it off his face*):   Why not?

(*The three others leap to their feet and surround her, menacingly.*)

Ruccioni (*with a gesture*):   No!... Leave her alone!... (*To Géméa*) So!... Do you know me?

Géméa: Your face and your name, my friend... Signor Ruccioni...

Ruccioni: How do you know?

Géméa (*pointing to the others*):   Send your friends away, and I'll tell you.

Ruccioni (*to the others, gesturing them out*):   You heard her...

Frimagusta (*to Ruccioni*):   Be careful, captain! It could be a trick...

(*Ruccioni waves them off.*)

Frigolini (*as Castara and Frimagusta exit, aside*):   Lucky I have this mask! If not, I bet she'd fire me, for sure!

(*He follows them out.*)

SCENE 2
Ruccioni, Géméa

Ruccioni: So... No need to deny it... Ruccioni at your service!... Eccentric, I admit... And something of a thief... But not a bad sort, all in all...

Géméa: Indeed...

Ruccioni: And an excellent soldier, if only I could take orders... (*With a little shrug*) Oh well... So, you know me, do you?

Géméa: Let's say I saw you once...

Ruccioni: Ah... And once is enough... Or too much, right?

Géméa: I seem to recall, you were leaving—

Ruccioni (*not letting her finish*):   A brothel?... Perhaps... Or a palace we were ransacking?... More likely... Or a dismal tavern, teeming with flesh, on some dark, godforsaken street?... Yes, probably... I do get drunk at least once a day... (*Inviting her to continue*) Sorry... You were saying?

Géméa: You were leaving the shipyards.

Ruccioni: Oh?... And when was that?

Géméa: Three years ago...

Ruccioni: Three years...?

Géméa: One night... After dark... With your cape over your arm...

Ruccioni: Ah yes... (*Recollecting*) But that night it wasn't the thief...
Not the pickpocket on the prowl... It was an honest worker!

Géméa: Oh?... A worker, wronged, and who was looking for justice?

Ruccioni: Exactly...

Géméa: A worker, looking for justice, and who was thrown out?

Ruccioni (*growing more intense*): Yes...

Géméa: A worker, thrown out, and who wanted revenge?

Ruccioni (*angrily*): Yes, damnation!... Yes, yes, yes!... And why stop?
There's more!... Why not add that it was a Lomellini who threw
me out?... A Lomellini who was my undoing...

Géméa (*softly*): I know...

Ruccioni: And that I still want my revenge!... Oh yes! How I want
it!

Géméa: Work for me and you shall have it!

Ruccioni: What?... In your hands?... My revenge?

Géméa: Yours, signore... And my own!

Ruccioni (growing interested): I'm listening... Tell me more...

Géméa: And ten thousand crowns for your trouble, my friend!

Ruccioni: Agreed!

Géméa: So be it!

(*There is a knock at the outside door.*)

Ruccioni (with a start): Who...?

Géméa (putting her finger to her lips): Shhh! (*Going to one of the windows and looking out, aside*) Ottavio! (*To Ruccioni, pointing to the door, down right*) In there, quick! And wait... Your fortune depends on it!

Ruccioni (moving to the door, aside): How, I wonder...

(*He exits, leaving the door slightly ajar and listening to what follows.*)

Géméa: Ottavio!... Here!... O God of Abraham, Isaac, and Jacob!... O God of vengeance!... You make this house a tribunal, and this wretched woman, a judge!

(*She opens the upstage door. Ottavio enters.*)

SCENE 3
Ottavio, Géméa

Géméa: You...

Ottavio: How pale you are, signora!

Géméa: With fear, do you think?

Ottavio: No, with hate...

Géméa: With hate?... Then why do you dare set foot in my home?

Ottavio: To speak calmly, signora...

Géméa (sarcastically):   To accuse me, calmly, of killing your mother?

(*Ottavio gives a start.*)

Ruccioni (hidden, aside):   Oh?...

Ottavio (to Géméa):   I come to you with an offer of peace.

Géméa: Go on...

Ottavio: I would like, if I can, to repair the wrong that my mother did you... I'm rich, need I tell you?

Géméa (with a sneer):   You needn't... And so?

Ottavio: Name your price...

Géméa: My price?

Ottavio: For leaving Genova, signora... (*Géméa shudders*) And never coming back...

Géméa: Leaving...?

Ottavio: Now... Tonight...

Géméa (controlling her emotion):   And where would you have me go?

Ottavio: As far as you like!

Géméa (looking him up and down):   Ah yes!... Then you know where my daughter is, my friend!

Ruccioni (aside):   Can it be?... She...

Géméa (to Ottavio):   You know that she is here... In Genova...

Ottavio: Nonsense!

Géméa: And you want to be rid of me... You know!... Yes, you know!

Ottavio: You're mad...

Géméa: Oh?... Then why do you care if I leave or if I stay? What difference can it make?

Ottavio: You...

Géméa (sarcastically):   How pale you are, count!... With fear, do you think?...

Ottavio (troubled):   No... I...

Géméa: And how upset you seem!

Ottavio: I...

Géméa: Let me give you some advice... If my enemies have sent you, turn them a deaf ear!... And if you know where my daughter is, then I beg of you, tell me!... For the love of God, tell me!... Give her back to her mother!...

Ruccioni (hidden, aside):   It must be...

Ottavio: Signora...

Ruccioni (aside):   She... Géméa...

(He continues listening intently.)

Géméa (*sighing*):   Ah... A desperate mother's pardon is as quick as her revenge... As quick and as complete!... I beg of you! Give her back...

Ottavio: It is not in my power!... No more than it is in yours to give me back my mother!

Géméa (*turning aside*):   Bah!...

Ottavio: Listen to me!... Please!... I have to speak... I have to tell you... I am trying to forestall a crime...

Géméa (*aside*):   What?

Ottavio: To cast out the two phantoms that hover over this chasm that divides us... The deadly phantoms of murder and revenge!

Géméa (*aside*):   He knows my plan...

Ottavio: Because to spill blood fills me with unspeakable horror!... Save me, signora! I cannot kill!... Save me from myself!

Géméa (*aside*):   Ha! I was wrong...

Ottavio: Now it is I who beg... Please! Leave!... No matter how much I tell myself... No matter how much I reason that even my mother would not blame you for her death... That you didn't know her condition... That she should have respected the sanctity of your home... Your child's home, signora...

Géméa: Ah...

Ottavio: That it was wrong not to leave her where God had placed her... With those chosen by Providence to care for her, to raise her... To leave her where she was born, in the cradle that her mother's love had blessed... (*Sighing*) No matter how much I say it, signora... I see you draw near, and my very soul rebels... I see my mother's shade loom up between us, and I hear her cry: "Revenge!"... Yes! I see her face, I hear her voice... Pressing me, urging me on... And I feel... I know that I must... (*Impassioned*) Please!... Listen to me! I beg you... Spare me this crime!... Leave Genova, I beg you!

Géméa: My blood fills you with fear... So much the better!

Ottavio: Yes, I admit it!... With fear and trembling... Fear for your threats to my happiness, to my love... Not fear for myself... Oh no! Not for me... I am not the one you would kill... I know that!... There are others you will choose... Others, whose suffering will cut me to the quick... Whose agony will kill me!

Géméa: Oh?

Ottavio: Yes... You have said as much... And I shudder to think... I know that my only salvation is to kill you!... But the thought of your blood on my hands, signora... No! Leave!... Leave!... You must...

Géméa: Fool!

Ottavio: I beg you! (*Falling to his knees*) For the love of God...

Géméa: Just as I begged your mother!

Ottavio: On my knees... I implore you...

Géméa: Just as I implored her!

Ottavio: For God's sake! Listen!... (*Beginning to weep*) Hear me! I beseech you...

Géméa (*gloating*):   Yes!... Beg! Beseech! Implore!... Each tear that you shed only strengthens my hate and hardens my revenge!

Ottavio (getting up):   Beast!

Géméa: I know now where to strike my blow!

Ruccioni (hidden, aside):   Ah...

(*Géméa pauses, as Ottavio looks deep into her eyes.*)

Ottavio: At Paola...? (*Nodding, as she remains silent*) At Paola...
(*Géméa gives him a cold, hard look in reply.*) Very well, then... (*Resigned*) A duel to the death, signora!... (*Intensely*) To the death!...
You hear me, woman?... "Woman"? Ah no! You are no woman!...
You... You monster!...

Géméa: So be it...

Ottavio: Not even a man could have made me tremble so!... Nothing human... You... You viper! (*As he strides toward the upstage door*)
Well, beware!... Oh yes... Beware!... I'll crush you underfoot if you
dare cross my path!

(*He exits. A moment later Ruccioni enters, down right.*)

SCENE 4
Géméa, Ruccioni

Géméa (to herself):   The lioness will have flesh to claw on in her grief!

Ruccioni (approaching her):   Your child, signora...

Géméa: You heard?

Ruccioni: You must have loved her very much!

Géméa: Loved her, you ask?

(*She begins to weep.*)

Ruccioni: To bear such hatred after all these years...

Géméa: God alone knows how I loved her!

Ruccioni (aside): Ah! The harm we do without ever thinking...

Géméa: So, Signor Ruccioni! My vengeance is yours!

Ruccioni: Years ago, I heard of your misfortune... Your grief...

Géméa: You?...

Ruccioni: I lived in Bisagno, in 1728... I even knew the godfather of your child, signora...

Géméa: You knew that wretch?

Ruccioni: That... Yes, I knew him... And well enough to know that he wished you no harm...

Géméa (with a sarcastic laugh): Oh?... How kind!... *(Fiercely)* Let God have mercy on his soul, signore!... His damnable soul!... I call down heaven's curse upon him!

Ruccioni (quite moved): And well you may... For a brigand like me, curses are empty words. A moment ago I would have laughed to hear you say them. But now I understand them, those words that condemn the... the wretch for what he did!... He deserves your curse, signora... I may be a brigand... I may have spent my life in rotting bordellos, with incredible trollops, and men worthy of dying like rats... Yes, I've fought with the police, and cheated at every table... And I've rifled my share of palaces, believe me!... But of all the crimes, of all the sins, the only one to tear at my heart is the one that caused your grief!

Géméa: My grief...? You...

Ruccioni (*realizing that he has said too much*):   I... I mean... To hear what you said... I... I couldn't help weeping! Just the thought, signora... The unspeakable thought that someone could snatch a poor babe from her mother's arms... Snatch her away, and give her to another... To turn her into a waif, a stray... Almost an orphan...

Géméa: Yes...

Ruccioni: Worse than a bastard!... A nobody...

Géméa: Then you accept?

Ruccioni (*continuing*):   Ah, signora... How I love you for loving your child so much! For being a mother!... When I think that I... that...

Géméa: And you will do my bidding?

Ruccioni (*continuing*):   ...that I could... that I was... Ah!... (*Replying*) Yes, yes... (*Holding out his hand*) Agreed!... And for nothing, dear woman!... My services are yours for the asking! Keep your gold!

Géméa (*shaking his hand*):   Good... (*Gesturing toward the upstage door*) Where are the others?... We shall need more than one for what I have in mind.

Ruccioni: For what you... You mean, you... You want me to have Ottavio killed?

Géméa: Killed?... Ha!... What kind of Italian are you, signore? Have you never learned to hate?... What is death, but one brief moment of suffering?... An agony quickly past...

Ruccioni (*somberly*):   Then... If I understand you... Yes, I would do anything in my power to help you find your child!... I would wear out my last pair of shoes if I had to!... But beyond that... No, signora... No...

Géméa: Ah...

Ruccioni: I used to think that mothers only wanted to lose their children!... You've proven me wrong, and I bless you for it!... But that's why Paola Lomellini will always be sacred to me... Yes, sacred... Because she has a mother too... A mother who would weep for her no less...

Géméa: Signore...

Ruccioni: Yes, I understand what you want... You would snatch that mother's child just as yours was snatched from you... You would torture another with your pain and your despair... You would... Ah no!... No, no!... One horror like that is enough! Too much!... Not even for twice your ten thousand crowns!... I'm not your man, signora!

Géméa (aside): O cursèd life of mine!...

Ruccioni: Farewell...

(*He turns to leave, upstage.*)

Géméa (aside): Even villains grow consciences rather than avenge me!

(*She sits down at the table.*)

Ruccioni (returning): I said that your tale made me weep, signora... Believe me, that's the truth... Even someone like me!... And I feel the better for it... Cleansed... As if the first tear washed the evil from my soul... (*Géméa stands up, impatiently, as if about to speak.*) No... Why should you care?... What can it matter to you how I feel?... But there's something you should know... I myself was a foundling... And because I was picked up in the street, like some stray dog, I wanted to bite at whatever came my way!... And I did! Once I was big enough and strong enough!... Oh yes!... Everyone and everything... Me against the world... Mean, vicious, unrelenting!... For more than twenty years...

Géméa: Signore...

Ruccioni (continuing):   And never in all those years... Not once, did I hope to find my mother... The one who gave me birth, but abandoned me where I lay... Sometimes I even wondered if my solitude, signora... If it was punishment from God... His wages for my sins... (*Géméa turns her back on him.*) Listen to me, please! Don't repeat the crimes of the brigand Ruccioni! Revenge is sweet today, but tomorrow its taste is bitter! It serves no purpose... It brings nothing back... God alone can give back to us what we have lost! Pray to Him... Perhaps he will give you back your daughter...

Géméa (in a whisper):   Perhaps...

Ruccioni: If, one day, He tells you: "This is your child!..." I promise you, if you find her... If you need the strong arm of a man to help you... Mine will be that arm! My arm, and my life! I swear it!... And nothing will keep me from bringing her to you... No fortress walls, no matter how high... Tooth and nail, I'll scale them and bring her back to her mother!

Géméa (sighing):   Ah...

Ruccioni: Until then, pray!... Godspeed, signora!

(*He exits, upstage.*)

SCENE 5
Géméa, alone

Géméa: "Revenge serves no purpose..." (*Musing*) How true... How true... And if I lift my hands to God in supplication... Criminal, sinful hands... How could He give me back my child? How could He listen to my prayers, steeped in blood?... And yet, for all these seventeen long years, I have prayed to Him with pure hands, unsullied by sin... I have choked back my cries, and swallowed my tears... Put aside my thoughts of vengeance in the hope that I might find her!... (*She crouches on the floor.*) God puts you to the test, Géméa!... Bow down before Him, and pray!... (*Raising her arms heavenward*) My God! My God!... God of Abraham, Isaac, and Jacob!... Look! I lay at your feet all the anger I have felt... I yield it up in sacrifice, God of Israel! God Almighty!... I lift up my suffering heart to you in prayer!... I beg you, my God! Hear me!... Give me back my child!... (*She pauses, weeping silently.*) Ah! Who knows if He hears me?... Who knows if He listens?... (*As she drops her arms to her sides, her hands touch some of the cards spread out on the floor.*) The cards... (*Picking them up*) Can they tell me?... What use have they been?... (*She begins dealing them out on the floor.*) Have they brought my Noémi back to my aching arms?... Lies! Lies!... Ah! God help me...

(*As she moves the cards about, Frigolini, again in his servant's garb, enters, upstage.*)

SCENE 6
Géméa, Frigolini

Frigolini (*stopping short*):   Ah...

(*He stands and watches her, unseen.*)

Géméa (*still dealing her cards, to herself*):   What's this?... Yesterday they told me she would die! And now... (*She deals them again, excitedly.*) What...?

Frigolini (*aside, with a shrug*):   If she's reading the cards, why not show the lady in?

(*He withdraws, as Géméa continues dealing her cards.*)

Géméa: Coming back?... Can it be?... (*She mixes them and deals again.*) Again?... My Noémi? Coming back?... (*Turning over a card, excitedly*) The Queen!... (*Exulting*) Thank God!... Thank God!... The first woman to cross my threshold...

Frigolini (*at the door, showing Bianca in, leaving the door open*):   Signora...

(*Bianca enters, veiled and gloved.*)

Géméa (*continuing, as Frigolini exits, down right*):   ... will bring back my child!... At last!... Back to my arms!

Bianca (*aside*):   God! Pardon my weakness...

Géméa (*continuing*):   And I shall see her... My Noémi!... And I'll kiss her... (*Getting up*) My God!... (*Clutching her chest*) How my heart is beating!... Pounding... Can it be true?... (*Turning, noticing Bianca*) Who...? (*Addressing her*) Signora?... What... (*Aside*) A woman!... (*Looking toward the upstage door*) The first...!

SCENE 7
Géméa, Bianca

Bianca: Pardon me, signora... I... Perhaps...

(*She turns to leave.*)

Géméa: No! Stay!... I insist... (*Aside*) And veiled!... Like the lady in the carriage!

Bianca (*reluctantly*):   If... If you're sure...

Géméa (*aside*):   Memories, how you haunt me!... (*To Bianca*) Do you come for a reading?

Bianca: Yes...

Géméa (aside):   How it pains me to remember... (*To Bianca*) Show me your hand, signora...

Bianca: My hand?... But... The cards...?

Géméa: Cards... Hands... I read them all! The powers of light have bestowed their gifts upon me... My soul is one with the past, and the future holds no secrets!... (*Reaching out with her left hand*) Come... Your hand... (*Bianca holds out her right hand.*) No, no... The left... Close to your heart... And ungloved, signora... (*As Bianca removes her glove, aside*) Can it be?... (*Taking her hand, invoking*) O powers of light, descend upon me!... (*Looking at the hand, aside*) A scar!... Good God! The hand that held the carriage door!...

(*She begins to tremble.*)

Bianca: You're trembling, signora...

Géméa: The spirits... The powers...

Bianca: And how pale you are!

Géméa: The forces, within me... Draining my strength... (*Aside*) Oh! The tortures of the past... (*To Bianca, in a commanding tone*) Your veil!... Lift it!

Bianca (hesitating):   But...

Géméa: You must! You must!... (*Bianca complies.*) So! Bianca Lomellini!

Bianca (with a gasp):   You... You know my name?

Géméa: I know everything! All there is to know!... Bianca, daughter of the last duke of L'Orioni... Wife of Giovanni Lomellini...

Whose wedding gift was the island of Taberca... "The Coral Isle"...

Bianca: But how...

Géméa (aside): And mother of Paola!... (*To Bianca*) Let the cards tell the rest!... (*Gesturing toward the table*) Sit down... Sit down...

Bianca (sitting in the chair facing left, trembling, aside): God forgive me!

(*Géméa picks up the cards and assembles them in two packs.*)

Géméa (holding out both): The tarot will not lie!... Choose!

Bianca (vacillating): I... Whichever you wish...

Géméa (sternly): No! Choose!

Bianca (pointing): Those...

Géméa: Good!... Good!... (*As she mixes the cards*) And you know me too?

Bianca: No... I—

Géméa (interrupting): But you know who I am... What I do...

Bianca: Yes... I—

Géméa: And my name?

Bianca: I... I know that they call you "The Fortune-teller"...

Géméa: Is that all?

Bianca (hesitating): And...

Géméa (glaring at her):   And "The Bloodsucker"?...

Bianca: Please, I—

Géméa: And "The Usurer"?...

Bianca: I have no time...

Géméa (presenting the deck to her):   Cut! (*As Bianca clumsily cuts the cards*) And you have never seen me?

Bianca: Never!... Please! Let's get on...

Géméa (slowly and deliberately):   All in due time... All in due time... (*She divides the deck into four piles.*) There!... (*Pointing*) Four piles... You see them?... One... Two... Three...

Bianca (growing more and more frustrated):   Yes!... Please, signora...

Géméa: Good!... (*Sitting down, facing the footlights*) At each of my questions, you choose one... Is that clear?

Bianca: Yes... Yes...

Géméa: Good...

(*She makes several mystical passes over the four piles.*)

Bianca (crossing herself, aside):   God help me!

Géméa: Is it for you the tarot will speak? You yourself...?

Bianca: Yes...

Géméa: So!... (*Pointing to the piles, sharply*) Choose!... (*Bianca points to one of the piles.*) Aha!... (*She takes the chosen pile and turns over the cards, one at a time, slowly and deliberately.*) All in due time...

(*Reading them*) I see many travels... Yes... Great distances... And much torment...

Bianca (*aside*):   Oh...

Géméa: Torment and despair... And pursued, as if stalked by some enemy... Or by some deep remorse... Or both... Ah yes, both... (*She picks up the cards, mixes them, and deals four piles again.*) A deep regret?... A feeling of guilt, for some sin committed...?

Bianca: No... I never—

Géméa (*pointing*):   Choose!

Bianca (*touching one of the piles*):   Ah...

Géméa (*dealing the cards again, reading them*):   So!... Again, your travels... With a babe in your arms... A child hidden from view... Clutched to your breast... (*Turning up a card*) Once you even fought to protect her!... Oh, how you fought!... Nearby... In La Polcevera... (*Turning up another*) From a woman... A desperate woman, who threw herself in front of your horses... (*Turning up another*) Clinging to the door of your carriage... (*Studying the cards intently*) And she scratches you... Digs her nails into your hand... (*Pointing to Bianca's hand, on the table*) There!... That scar, perhaps... (*As Bianca quickly withdraws her hand, aside*) Her!... Now I know!

Bianca (*aside*):   What kind of witch... (*To Géméa*) I've never been in La Polcevera...

Géméa: Oh?... Perhaps not... (*As she picks up the cards*) And yet... Perhaps... (*Dealing out the four piles*) Are you afraid of the truth, signora?

Bianca: Certainly not!

Géméa (*pointing to the cards*):   Choose!... (*Bianca points to a pile.*) It is for the cards to answer!... (*Again, turning the cards over, slowly*) Yes... A disaster, hanging over you... Worse... Ruin!... (*Turning another card, louder*) Utter ruin!... (*Turning another, louder still*) Complete and utter ruin...

Bianca (*aside*):   Good God!

Géméa: Unless... (*Turning another*) Ah, yes!... You can be saved...

Bianca: Saved...?

Géméa (*studying the cards*):   By a woman... A Gypsy, or a Moor... One you have seen, or will see, this very day... Perhaps even a Jewess...

Bianca: And...?

Géméa (*turning another card*):   Ah!... I see much uncertainty in your household!... This card... A living being... But look... Turned upside down!... The sign of confusion... The sign of mourning...

Bianca (*anxiously*):   A death...?

Géméa: No, no... (*Turning another card*) Living... Alive... A daughter... (*Bianca gives a start.*) You have a daughter?

Bianca: Yes...

Géméa (*studying the cards laid out on the table*):   Your daughter... But...

Bianca: But what?... Tell me...

Géméa: Strange...

Bianca: What do you see? What is it?

Géméa (*shaking her head*):   Very strange...

Bianca: I want to know!... I must...

Géméa: And you have never been separated from this daughter of yours?

Bianca: Never!

Géméa: Perhaps... Even when she was nursing?

Bianca: I nursed her myself!

Géméa: You?... A countess...?

Bianca: Yes!

Géméa: You nursed this child yourself?

Bianca: I did!... I did!...

Géméa (looking squarely at her): Woe unto those who lie to me!... Who lie to the cards...

Bianca: But...

Géméa: Remember Muranotti!... He lied, and now he is dead!

Bianca: Why do you tell me this?

Géméa: The tarot have spoken!... That child is waiting... Waiting for her mother!

Bianca (getting up): But I am her mother!

Géméa: You?... A countess? A duchess?... Your blood is not her blood, my noble friend! Hers is a humble birth... Her race, a race reviled... Not yours...

Bianca: That's not true, I tell you!

Géméa: You are a Christian!... (*With a gesture toward the outspread cards*) And she is a Jew!

Bianca: Enough of your lying!... I'll not have it, do you hear?... Your cards tell you nothing!... My enemies... (*Trembling*) It is my enemies who have told you what to say!

Géméa: Oh?

Bianca: You lie! You lie!

Géméa (*sarcastically*):   I lie? And yet you tremble?... I lie? Yet you grow pale?... Will I lie too when I tell you what has brought you to see me?... Why you seek my services...?

Bianca: Enough!... (*Turning to leave*) I'll hear no more!

Géméa (*jumping up, standing in her way*):   You will!... You must!... It is not only "The Fortune-teller's" services that you seek!... It is "The Usurer's"!

Bianca: Me?

Géméa: The one who can help you to restore your crumbling fortune...!

Bianca: But...

Géméa: The one who can buy your husband's freedom from his captors...!

Bianca (*aside*):   Good God! She knows everything!

Géméa (*crossing left, and opening a secret compartment in one of the ar-*

moires left open by the thieves, revealing huge piles of gold):   See?...
The ransom is here!... Look at it, my friend!

Bianca (*overwhelmed at the sight*):   Oh!...

Géméa: Gold enough to buy palaces... Enough to buy a city...

Bianca: But...

Géméa: A few moments ago, thieves invaded my home. And what
did they find? Not a thing!... For them it was nothing but a poor,
empty hovel!... For you... (*With a grand gesture toward the gold*) For
you, it is the richest of palaces, signora!

Bianca (*deciding to admit her mission*):   Ah, yes... Yes... I'll not deny
why I have come...

Géméa (*with a sarcastic smile*):   And even if you will...

Bianca (*continuing*):   Yes! You can save us!... If only you would...

Géméa: Go on...

Bianca: My husband is held prisoner by the bey of Tunis... I must
have his ransom, signora...

Géméa: A tidy sum, no doubt...

Bianca: And even more!... To pay his debts... Foolish debts to this
one and that... (*Desperately*) Oh! I beg you!... You can give us back
our honor, our good name!... You can save my husband's life!

Géméa (*coldly*):   No doubt...

Bianca: Besides, you take no risk... You know the Lomellini fortune!... We have a galley in the Indies, and two more, rented to

the king of Spain... Yours to hold against the loan... I have seen to everything... (*She takes a document from her reticule and holds it up.*) The agreement is drawn and signed... With my signature, signora...

Géméa: So I see...

Bianca: Ah! I beg you!... Save our honor!... Save my husband!... I beg you!

Géméa: Your terms are unacceptable.

Bianca: What?

Géméa: Your pledges are insufficient.

Bianca: Then take my diamonds, signora... My villa... (*Géméa gives a disdainful wave of the hand.*) My palaces... Both of them...

Géméa: Not enough...

Bianca: Not... But my God! How much more...? What else can I give you?

Géméa: One word!... A single word... Yes or no... Is Paola your daughter?

Bianca: Paola...? What difference can it make to you?

Géméa: Ah! I too have my pride!... Pride in my craft, my science... Pride in my knowledge of the tarot, in their message... So! Is she your daughter?

Bianca: Oh!

Géméa (*gesturing*):   Gold, signora...

Bianca: God help me!

Géméa: Yours... If only you answer...

Bianca (*aside*):   Can I trust her with my secret?

Géméa: Tomorrow may be too late...

Bianca (*aside*):   What if they take her from me?

Géméa (*with another gesture toward the gold*):   Your husband's ransom!... And more!

Bianca: Ah!... Giovanni!... How can I forsake you?... Abandon you... Leave you to die...

Géméa (*insisting*):   Is she your daughter?

Bianca (*torn between her two emotions*):   Please... I...

Géméa: I must know!

Bianca (*reluctantly*):   If you promise they'll not take her from me...

Géméa (*with a cry of victory*):   Aha!... Then the cards were right! She is not your child!... And her mother... Her poor, wretched mother...

Bianca: Will she try to reclaim her?... Tell me, please!... Do you know her?

Géméa: Know her?... Oh yes, I know her!... Her name is Géméa!... (*With a victorious smile*) My name, signora!... I am her mother!

Bianca (*shocked*):   You?

Géméa: And my joy did not betray me!... After searching all these years...

Bianca: It was a trap!

Géméa (*jubilant*):   All my suffering, all my pain!... Gone, in an instant!...

Bianca: A vicious trap!

Géméa (*not listening to her, pointing to the gold*):   Take it!... Take it all!... Handfuls... Armfuls... As much as you like... My child is the only wealth I need!

Bianca: Keep your vile gold! I'll seek help from other quarters!

Géméa: As you wish, signora... Do as you please! So long as you give me back my child!

Bianca: Never!

Géméa: What?... Take care! I'm warning you... Now that I know...

Bianca: Never! You hear?... Never!

Géméa: I'll drag you before the courts!

Bianca: I'll deny every word!

Géméa: And your conscience?

Bianca: It will be stilled, I assure you!

Géméa: You mean, you would dare...?

Bianca: For my daughter...

Géméa: *My* daughter!... You would dare hide the truth? You would perjure yourself?

Bianca: Gladly!

Géméa (*going to the upstage door, closing it, and standing in front of it*):   Then you'll not leave this house!

Bianca: You... (*Raising her voice*) You witch! You sorceress!... Open that door!

Géméa: Only when you send word to Paola to come join me... To come to her mother! (*She points to the inkwell, quill, and paper on the table.*) Write!

Bianca: No!

Géméa (*pushing her toward the table*):   Write, I said!

Bianca: Never!

Géméa: So be it!

(*She puts on her cloak.*)

Bianca: Where are you going?

Géméa: My heart is all I need to convince my Noémi!

Bianca (*standing at the door, barring her way, shouting*):   Oh? I think not!...

Géméa (*shouting*):   Stand aside!...

Bianca: Vile Jewess!

Géméa: Stand aside, I tell you!

(*As Bianca persists, she seizes her and pushes her out of the way, and flings her to the ground.*)

Bianca: Ayyy!

(*Frigolini, attracted by the noise, comes running in, down right.*)

Géméa (*to Frigolini, pointing to Bianca*):   Guard her, Frigolini!... I leave her in your care!

(*She exits, upstage.*)

CURTAIN

Act 3

A small bedchamber in the Lomellini palace, elegantly furnished. A door, down right, and a casement window in the side wall, up left. Against the upstage wall, a canopied bed with a small table beside it, right. On the table, a lamp. Against the wall, down left, a small shrine with a prie-dieu in front of it. On the wall behind it, a large crucifix. Down left, a table, with flowers, a book, and an embroidery basket. Near the table, two armchairs, close to each other, one with a cushion at the foot of it. Other appropriate furnishings, *ad libitum*.

At rise, it is early morning. The sun's rays are coming through the window. The lamp on the bedside table is lit.

SCENE 1
Teresa, alone

Teresa (obviously upset, pacing nervously): But wherever can she be?... Gone!... Disappeared!... And first thing in the morning... And Paola, poor child!... Here, a moment ago, looking for her mother... Desperate... Weeping bitter tears... I felt like telling her: "Don't worry, my dear! She's not really your mother anyway! We've lied to you all these years!..." But that probably would have killed her!

(*Ottavio enters.*)

SCENE 2
Ottavio, Teresa

Ottavio (running up to Teresa, up left, by the window): What's this I hear?... The duchess...

Teresa: Gone, signore!... No one knows where she is!... I came in the minute the sun came up... To wake her... (*With a gesture around the room*) And she was gone!

Ottavio: Is anyone looking for her?

Teresa: Everyone in the palace!

Ottavio: And Paola...?

Teresa: She's run off to the Carmelite convent. I thought her mother might have gone there... To pray for... (*Stopping, circumspectly*) The count knows, I'm sure...

Ottavio: About her husband?... Of course I do!

Teresa: Well, I didn't tell her why, but I thought maybe Signora Lomellini would be praying...

Ottavio: I've already sent the ransom...

Teresa (*hearing footsteps approaching*):   Shhh!... I think that's Paola... (*Whispering*) Not a word about how concerned you are... No need to worry the poor child even more...

(*Paola enters, pale and trembling.*)

SCENE 3
Ottavio, Teresa, Paola

Paola (*to herself, taking no notice of the others*):   Not there!... God in heaven! Where can she be? (*Taking off her shawl*) I... I know that something simply frightful has happened!... I feel myself dragged toward the edge of a chasm... A horrible abyss... By some unseen force... (*She goes to the shrine and kneels down, praying.*) My God! My God!... Please watch over my mother!

(*She continues her prayer, sotto voce.*)

Teresa (approaching, as Paola crosses herself):   Signorina...

Paola (looking up):   Oh...

Teresa: Count Ottavio is here.

Paola (getting up, to Ottavio):   My mother, Ottavio... She... She's disappeared!

Ottavio (trying to calm her):   Now, now...

Paola (pointing):   Her bed is still made!... (*To Teresa*) Her lamp has been burning all night, Teresa!

Teresa: When I saw her last evening she was perfectly fine...

Paola (to Ottavio):   I went running to the Carmelites... Teresa thought...

Teresa (continuing):   In fact, I remember... She was smiling when she told me I could retire for the night...

Paola (continuing):   For a moment I thought I saw her in the street... Suddenly I was so relieved... My heart was pounding, and already my arms were reaching out to embrace her... But no! It wasn't... It was someone else... Oh! Ottavio! Ottavio!... If my mother has come to grief... If anything has happened to her... It will be the death of me, Ottavio!

Teresa (trying to calm her):   Now, now... There's no need... More than likely she's with some friend... On an errand of mercy...

Paola: Ah! Yes... Of course!... The princess Belmori... She's been ill for two days! Why didn't I think of it? My mother must be... Yes, of course... (*To Teresa*) Be a dear, Teresa...

Teresa: Signorina?

Paola: Run and see... As if you were simply passing by... I don't want her to think... Then hurry back and tell me... (*Gesturing toward the door*) Quickly! Quickly!

(*As Teresa turns to leave, there is a loud knock at the outside door.*)

Teresa: The door, signorina...

Paola: Yes... First see who that can be...

(*Teresa exits.*)

Ottavio: Really, Paola, my dear... There's no need to worry... You're much too concerned! A Lomellini doesn't simply disappear!... And certainly not a duchess!

Paola: No... Of course not... You're right... But I'll not have a moment's peace until she takes me in her arms!

Teresa (*entering, to Paola*): Signorina... There's a gentleman... A stranger... He says he must speak with you. He says it's important.

Paola: A stranger?

Ottavio (*to Teresa*): What does he look like?

Teresa: Like an upstart, if you ask me...

Paola: Perhaps he knows... (*To Teresa*) Show him in...

Ottavio (*to Paola*): If you think...

(*He withdraws upstage, out of sight, as Teresa exits momentarily, then shows in Ruccioni.*)

SCENE 4
Ottavio, Paola, Teresa, Ruccioni

Paola (*to Ruccioni, joining him, anxiously*):   Signore... You come with a message from the duchess, no doubt!

Ruccioni: No, signorina.

Paola: But... But you know where she is!... Tell me...

Ruccioni: I'm afraid not...

Paola (*to Teresa*):   Quick!... To the princess Belmori!...

Teresa: Very good...

(*Teresa exits.*)

Paola (*to Ruccioni*):   What is it you wish?

Ruccioni: To save you...

Ottavio (*aside*):   What?

Paola: Me?... Save me...? From what?

Ruccioni: At your age, signorina, you should have no enemies... But you do! Believe me!... And vicious ones...

Paola: Enemies...?

Ruccioni: No matter what anyone says... Even if they tell you that the palace is on fire... That it's falling to the ground... Promise me that you'll not leave these walls!

Paola: Whatever for?

Ruccioni: Even if they tell you that your mother is in danger... Or your betrothed... No matter... You must not leave this palace... At least, not without a brave man at your side... The one who will be your husband, signorina, and who will protect you if need be... Count Ottavio...

Paola: But signore...

Ruccioni: I have no more to say. Godspeed, signorina...

(*He turns to leave.*)

Paola (*stopping him*):   But these enemies... Who are they?

Ruccioni: Never fear... I'll be on guard...

Paola: You say you want to save me... But I'm only half safe unless I know their names.

Ruccioni: No... I've said all I can... From this moment on, I'm your shadow, signorina. When there's danger, I'll be there. When it's past, I'll disappear. You'll not even have to trouble to thank me!

Paola: But...

Ruccioni: That's how I am... (*With a little bow*) Your obedient servant... Devoted, but out of sight...

(*He turns again to leave.*)

Ottavio (*coming downstage, confronting him*):   One moment!... I'll have a word...

Ruccioni: Ah!... Signor Ottavio...

Ottavio (*holding out a purse*):   A hundred ducats... But you must earn them...

Ruccioni: By naming names, no doubt... (*Refusing the purse with a gesture*) Ah, but when one must hold his tongue... Thank you, but no... Your purse holds a question that I cannot answer, count.

Ottavio: And the reason?

Ruccioni: There is one. Let that suffice...

Ottavio: A reason that refuses to listen to reason?

Ruccioni: Well put!

Ottavio: Then perhaps it will listen to the sword, my friend!

Ruccioni: Even less, I'm afraid!

Ottavio: Oh? You think so?... (*Drawing his sword in a false show of bravado*) By God! You'll speak!... Even if I have to kill you...

Ruccioni (*drawing his*):   By God! Then you'll have to kill me first! My lips are sealed...

Paola (*stepping quickly between them, to Ottavio*):   Ottavio! Please!... (*To Ruccioni*) Signore... (*Throwing her arms around his neck, as Ottavio, grumbling, withdraws upstage*) I beg you...

Ruccioni (*sheathing his sword*):   Bah!... (*To himself*) Fool! You almost undid your good deed!

Paola (*to Ruccioni*):   He's wrong... Forgive him... I understand...

Ruccioni (*turning to leave*):   Well...

Paola (*stopping him, throwing her arms around his neck again*):   No, please... Stay, signore! I... I need your help!

Ruccioni: When you put it that way, you could make me your slave!

Paola:　You've saved the daughter... Now I ask you to save the mother!

Ruccioni:　Yours?

Paola:　Mine!... My enemies... The ones you speak of... They must be hers too! She... She has disappeared!

Ruccioni:　What?

Paola:　The danger that was threatening me must have struck at her instead!

Ruccioni (aside):　Damnation! (*To Paola*) Disappeared, you say?... Your mother...? (*Aside*) Could it be that Géméa has...

Paola:　I ask you to name no names, my friend... Keep your secrets to yourself, but save my mother! I beg you! That's all I ask...

Ruccioni (aside):　I wonder...

Paola:　Why, I cannot say... But I trust you, signore... I feel certain that you can help me, and I know that you will!... You are good, I can tell... (*Sobbing softly*) Oh, please! I beg you! Let your heart hear my prayer!...

Ruccioni (touched):　Signorina...

Paola:　Reach out to this poor child, who is looking for her mother... Have pity on her... (*Falling to her knees*) I beg you!... Find her... Find her, and bring her back!

(*She continues sobbing, as Ruccioni, awkwardly, tries to comfort her.*)

Ruccioni (raising her up finally):　Please... You? At my feet...? Really... That's not right... (*Aside*) I must be dreaming...

Paola: You will find her?... Tell me you will, signore...

Ruccioni (*determined*):   Yes! If it's possible... (*With a second thought*) And yes, even if it's not!

Paola: Oh...

Ottavio (*approaching them*):   Do you know where she is?

Ruccioni: I may...

Ottavio (*extending his hand*):   Can you use a friend to help?

Ruccioni: A good sword never hurts!... Come... (*Taking his hand*) Follow me... (*Shaking it*) Friend!

Ottavio (*to Paola*):   Hope, Paola... And pray!

Ruccioni (*to Paola*):   Godspeed, signorina!

(*He and Ottavio go hurrying off.*)

SCENE 5
Paola, alone

Paola (*sighing*):   Ah... That man... He'll help me, I know it!... Suddenly I'm at peace... I know that he'll find her! I know that my mother will come back to me!... She will! She will!... She's coming... I can feel it...

(*Géméa appears in the doorway. She stops short as if stunned at the sight of Paola.*)

SCENE 6
Géméa, Paola

Géméa (*overcome, aside*):   Ah!... Noémi...

Paola (without noticing her, continuing):   And when she does, I want her to see that I've thought only of her...

(She picks up the prayer book from the table.)

Géméa (aside):   My child...

Paola (continuing):   Each of these prayers is still moist with my tears!... (*Kissing the book*) Holy tears!... Blessèd tears!... Tears that have taught me how much I love my mother...

(She lays the book on the prie-dieu in front of the shrine.)

Géméa (aside):   Can it be...?

Paola (arranging the things on the table):   Her flowers...

Géméa (aside):   How she's grown!... But I knew...

Paola (continuing):   Her embroidery...

Géméa (aside):   I saw her grow every time I closed my eyes!... Saw her in my heart...

Paola (arranging one of the chairs, continuing):   Her chair... And her cushion, for me to sit on at her feet...

Géméa (aside):   A vision... A vision...

Paola (wiping her eyes, good-naturedly, continuing):   Oh, how I'll scold her for making me weep these tears!... Naughty thing!...

(She goes to place the prayer book on the prie-dieu.)

Géméa (reaching out to her, softly):   My child... My Noémi...

Paola (noticing her, drawing back):   Oh!...

Géméa (tenderly):   I'm here... I've come...

Paola (frightened):   You!... (*Aside*) Good God!... That woman... Last night...

Géméa: Noémi...

Paola (looking about, aside):   And no one to help me... (*Calling*) Teresa!... Teresa!...

Géméa: No, no!... Please!...

Paola: But... What do you want?... Who are you?... (*As Géméa approaches*) Stay away!... Stay... (*Calling*) Teresa!

Géméa: Please!... I'm not going to hurt you... (*Falling to her knees*) See?... I beg of you...

Paola: But... Whatever for, signora?... Why...

Géméa (sighing):   Ah!... Misery me!...

Paola: What is it?... What...

Géméa: See?... No longer do you fear me... See?

Paola (moving to raise her to her feet):   Fear you?... No, signora... I... (*Compassionately*) I pity anyone in distress...

Géméa (aside):   She touched me!...

Paola (raising her up):   Please... (*Leading her to one of the chairs*) Come... Sit down...

Géméa: Oh... How happy you make me!... How happy, my child... (*She sits down, gazing at her.*) And how beautiful you are!... Yes... So beautiful... And so good, so kind...

(*She begins weeping.*)

Paola: But... My poor friend... Why are you weeping?

Géméa: Why?... (*Sighing*) Ah... Why... (*Aside*) How do I tell her? How do I begin?

Paola: Is there something I can do?...

Géméa (*aside*):   How do I tell her: "My child, I am your mother!"

Paola (*continuing*):   Anything that would ease your pain?

Géméa (*trembling, aside*):   That word... "Mother"...

Paola (*continuing*):   There must be something... The poor stranger in our house is a guest sent by God! You tell me that I am kind, signora... And, tender as I am, that makes me wish to be even kinder!... Come, tell me... What can I do for you?... Please... (*She sits down in the other chair.*) We must talk... Just the two of us... How can I help you?

Géméa (*aside*):   My life is in her hands... (*To Paola, hesitating*) I... I...

Paola: Surely you cannot distrust me...

Géméa: Oh, no!... How could I?... You... You, my...

Paola: Then tell me... Please! Speak to me, as your friend...

Géméa (*pathetically, aside*):   My friend...

Paola: Never will you find a heart more easily moved than mine... More ready to share your woes...

Géméa (*reaching out*):   Give me your hand...

Paola: My hand?... (*Hesitating*) But...

Géméa: Please... It will bring me luck...

Paola: If you wish...

(*She holds out her hand to her.*)

Géméa: I do... I do... (*Taking her hand in hers*) When we suffer... Oh, how superstitious we become!... You see, I... I'm looking for a lost child... My daughter, signorina...

Paola (*with a note of pity*):   How frightful...

Géméa: And she would be so much like you... So very, very much... But they took her from me!

Paola: Oh...

Géméa: If I hold your hand in mine, it's her hand that I touch... If I press your fingers to my lips, it's her fingers that I kiss...

(*She covers Paola's hand with kisses.*)

Paola: I understand... Oh, I do... (*Aside*) Poor soul!... And to think I feared her!... (*To Géméa, tenderly*) You say that your daughter was taken from you, signora?

Géméa: As a child...

Paola: And you never saw her again?

Géméa: Yes, once... Only once... After seventeen years!

Paola: Did she know you?

Géméa: Ask your heart, signorina... What does your heart tell you?

Paola: It says that she must have known you! The minute she saw
you!... No matter how long... (*Excitedly*) How could she fail to...
Her soul must have jumped, must have bounded to greet yours!

Géméa (*sighing*):   Ah...

Paola: Her arms must have opened to clutch you to her bosom!

Géméa (*sadly*):   Not so, my child...

Paola: No?... How can that be?... We are joined soul to soul, as well
as blood to blood!... I know that my soul would have leapt to join
my mother's!

Géméa (*aside*):   Alas...

(*She begins sobbing softly.*)

Paola: What is it?... Tell me...

Géméa: Nothing, my child... Nothing... So often I weep without
even knowing why...

Paola (*trying to distract her*):   Your daughter... What was her name?

Géméa: Her name?... (*Watching her, hoping for a reaction*) Noémi...
Yes, her name was Noémi... (*Disheartened at Paola's lack of response*)
But she has another now... A Christian name, signorina...

Paola: Oh?

Géméa: To separate us even more!... It was not enough merely to
take her from me!... They had to place a foreign God between us...

Paola (*gently*):   The true God, signora...

Géméa: The God that drives her from me!

Paola: Then your daughter is a Christian?

Géméa: Alas!... (*Observing her carefully*) A wealthy Christian lady claimed to be her mother...

Paola: And she believed her?

Géméa: How could she not?

Paola: Then surely she must love her...

Géméa: And you?... Would you love her if you were in her place?

Paola: How frightful!... To be torn between love for two mothers... The one that nature gave her, and the other... Mere chance!

Géméa: But I am the one she should love!... I alone...

Paola: You speak as my own dear mother would speak!

Géméa (aside):   Her mother!... (*Standing up, with a sudden outburst*) Ha!... So, you love that woman, do you?... You love her so much?

(*She turns her back and moves up right.*)

Paola (standing up):   That woman?... Her?... (*Uncomprehending*) Who...?

Géméa (turning to her):   The duchess Lomellini!

Paola (joining her):   My mother?... (*Confused*) You ask if I love my mother?... But... How can you doubt it? You, who know what it is to love!... You, who love your daughter so!

Géméa (aside):   Good God! I'll go mad!

Paola: Why, this very morning... You hear?... This morning, I awoke, brimming with happiness... Not a care in the world... Life was singing in my heart. Even the pale ray of sunlight that roused me from my sleep seemed ready to share my joy... I dressed and came tiptoeing here, into my mother's room, to surprise her with a kiss... Happy... Smiling... But all of a sudden the smile froze on my lips. (*With a gesture about the room*) The room was empty! She was gone!... Disappeared!... I grew weak... My heart stood still!... I would have died, I'm sure of it, if not for a kind man... A stranger, who reassured me...

Géméa (*aside*):   Ah...

Paola (*continuing*):   Died, I tell you!... I would have, I know it!... And yet, you would ask me if I love her, signora? (*Impassioned*) Tell me, how could I not?... How?

Géméa (*aside*):   God help me!

Paola (*continuing*):   Not love her?... Impossible!... Everyone does! She's so good, so sweet, so kind... Do you know her? Do you know how beautiful she is?... Like a Raphael madonna!... So lovely, signora... Oh! What a frightful rival she would be! Too lovely for words...

Géméa: It's easy to be lovely when one has never suffered!

Paola: Never suffered?... My mother?... Oh! How wrong you are! She suffered more than I can tell you! And for me, signora!... Me... Some children are born to thrive... To open their petals to the sun, like flowers... But I... No... I was weak and frail... A glimmer of life, a wisp of breath... My soul, my life were floating away... Each day I would seem to be dying a little more... All the care of a mother was still not enough! What she gave me, signora, was the devotion of an angel! The self-sacrifice, the patience... And you ask me if I love her?

Géméa (*aside*):   I should have been the one...

Paola: For five years she struggled against death itself to save me... Wrapped me in all the tenderness of her heart... She filled my days and nights with her presence... And little by little all my ills disappeared, all my suffering ceased. It was only her love that snatched me from the grave!... And you ask me if I love her?

Géméa (sighing, aside):   Ah!... Never will she love me then... (*Weeping*) Why should she...

Paola: But... You're weeping, my friend...

Géméa (dejected, turning to leave):   Farewell, signorina...

Paola (stopping her):   No! Please!... Don't go!... You fascinate me...

Géméa (despairing):   Me? So unlike a Raphael madonna?... So ugly?... Ah... (*Musing*) The voice of the blood, they tell us... The voice of nature... Oh! What lies!... What abominable lies!

Paola (uncomprehending):   Signora?

Géméa: Nature and blood are silent!... No voice but the blood of seventeen years, together... (*To herself*) What now, Géméa?... Poor childless mother!... No future but the tomb!... (*To Paola*) Farewell!... (*Turning to go*) Farewell, sweet child... My house... Still empty... And empty will it be when death comes to claim me! No crowd about my coffin... They will carry me off, like a useless, pathetic thing... And that will be the end... (*Sarcastically*) What a joy this life of ours!... Farewell, my child...

Paola (stopping her):   No... I beg you! I'll not let you leave this way...

Géméa: Ah, yes... You are good, you are kind... And I thank you!... You give me as much of your heart as you are able.

Paola: Please!... If only you would tell me your troubles...

Géméa: No, no... It is done...... (*Calmly*) My soul boils up at times, and overflows... But now, it is done... Finished... No more...

Paola: But perhaps I can help...

Géméa: Help?... Yes... If one day we meet, try not to flee in horror or turn aside in disgust! A kind word will be like alms!... And if, by chance, you cast a smile at my feet... Ah! How quickly shall I gather it up!... That smile will light my shadows, signorina, and it will bless the darkness of my days!

Paola (*touched*): Oh...

Géméa: Do you promise?

Paola: Yes!... I do! I do!

Géméa: Then, again, I thank you... (*Turning to leave*) And again, farewell...

(*Taking only a step or two. she stops, utters a piercing cry, and collapses onto one of the chairs.*)

Paola (*alarmed*): Oh!

Géméa: My God!... How can I...?

Paola (*trembling, aside*): That cry!...

Géméa (*to Paola*): How can I leave you?... (*To herself*) After seventeen years... (*Looking heavenward*) Help me!... (*Sobbing*) God help me!

Paola (*going to her*): Signora! What is it?... Please! What's troubling you?

Géméa: Troubling me...? I... Paola Lomellini, I... (*Standing up, de-*

termined) I am your mother!... (*Paola jumps back, agape and transfixed, listening as she continues.*) Your mother!... Yes!... Standing here, before you!... The mother who lost you... The mother whose babe they stole from her cradle... You... You are that child!... My Noémi!... You, whose poor father died of grief!...

Paola: Signora...

Géméa (*continuing*): Yes, this seems like a dream... I know... You can hardly believe your ears! Why should you?... But how can I not tell you the truth?... I must, I have no choice... I know, I know... You think me nothing but a miserable fortune-teller!... Ah, yes!... But why? Why did I learn the tarot?... One reason and only one, my child!... To make the cards tell me if I would ever find you... To read my own fate...

Paola (*compassionately*): My friend...

Géméa (*continuing*): How droll, that I should read others' fortunes too!... Ah! One day you will listen to all the tales I have to tell... So many... And how we will laugh, you and I!... Surrounded in luxury, wanting for nothing... (*Paola gives her a quizzical look*) Ah, yes! You think I am a pauper!... A wretched old hag!... (*As Paola is about to object*) Well, I am not!... I am rich!... Beyond your wildest dreams!... Millions!... Millions!... Come with me, and you will leave this palace for a palace richer still!... With huge marble columns, waiting to welcome you!... Your life will be a fairy tale! Your slightest wishes, granted!... Footmen by the score, at your beck and call... And beneath your feet, the finest Turkish carpets... And Venetian damask to drape over your shoulders...

Paola (*gently, as Géméa grows more and more impassioned*): Please...

Géméa: Everything!... Anything!... Whatever you wish!... All of Genova would be yours, if only it were for sale!... Ah! Noémi!... My Noémi!... I am your mother!... Come with me, my child...

Paola (with great pity, aside):   Utterly mad, poor thing...

Géméa: Quickly... Before they come and snatch you up again!... Oh! Come... Come with me...

Paola (trying to humor her):   Yes... Of course... Tomorrow...

Géméa (doubtful):   Oh...?

Paola: Tomorrow... Later...

Géméa (with a cry of utter despair):   God in heaven! She thinks I'm mad!... (*To Paola, reaching out to her*) Noémi!... My Noémi!... Believe me...

Paola (aside):   Poor soul! (*To Géméa*) Later... Later...

Géméa (raising her eyes to heaven):   My God! How could you...? After all I have suffered...

(*Ruccioni enters.*)

SCENE 7
Géméa, Paola, Ruccioni, Ottavio, Bianca

Ruccioni (to Paola):   The duchess, lovely lady...

(*Bianca and Ottavio appear in the doorway. As Géméa sees them, she draws back, far left.*)

Paola (to Bianca, rushing to greet her):   Mother!

Bianca (embracing her):   Ah! Paola!... My Paola!...

Paola: Mother!... Dearest!... (*To Ruccioni*) Oh! Thank you, signore!...

Géméa (aside):   We shall see, my friends!

Paola (to Ruccioni, continuing):   I knew I could trust you!... I knew...

Géméa (aside):   Ah, yes! We shall see!

Paola (to Ottavio):   Thank you, Ottavio!... Thank you, my belovèd!

(*Paola and Bianca come center, still embracing.*)

Paola (to Bianca):   It's you!... It is! It is!... Oh, how I've wept for you!... How I've worried...

Bianca (suddenly noticing Géméa):   Her!... (*Pointing*) Géméa!

Ottavio (still at the doorway):   That woman!... (*To Ruccioni, in a whisper*) See to it that no one enters!

(*Ruccioni nods assent and exits.*)

Paola (to Bianca):   You know her?

Bianca (to Ottavio):   The horses, Ottavio!... We're leaving the city at once! (*To Paola*) Come...

(*She and Paola move to leave.*)

Géméa (still far left, to Bianca, with a note of sarcasm):   But surely you'll not leave without me, signora?

Bianca (stopping):   Good God!

SCENE 8
Géméa, Bianca, Paola, Ottavio

Paola (to Bianca):   What does she mean?... Why is she staring at you so?...

Bianca: Please...

Paola: Who is she?

Bianca: No... Please, I...

Paola (*to Ottavio, pointing at Géméa*): Who is she?

Bianca (*embracing her*): No, no... You must not ask...

Paola (*breaking away, aghast, aside*): Ah!... Is it possible...? (*Aloud*) Tell me!... Someone! Tell me!

Ottavio: That vile creature was holding your mother prisoner... Why? Who can say?... (*Pointing at Géméa*) Look at her! She doesn't even bear the pallor of her wickedness!... (*To Géméa, approaching her*) I asked you... Man though I am, I begged you on bended knee... I pleaded that you not put my anger to the test!... And what do I find?... You! Here, in this house!... You, threatening the life of this child, my betrothed!... And the freedom of this woman, who will soon become my mother!...

Géméa (*coldly*): So be it...

Ottavio (*excitedly*): What?... You dare stand there, brazen as a statue? Looking us in the eye?... Glaring at us?... And you think I'll not be quick to take revenge?... You think I'll not strike you down?... Strike you dead?... Beware! Beware, I tell you!... (*Pointing to his sheathed dagger*) Much though I hate to shed blood, you foul crone... A few steps, and this dagger will forget my distaste!

Géméa (*to Bianca, calmly*): Signora... Please be so kind as to inform the count that we can do without his presence, and that we have much to discuss, you and I...

Ottavio (*approaching her, furiously*): You...! I thought I told you I would crush you underfoot if you dared cross my path!

Géméa: As you wish, count...

Paola (*trembling, clutching at her head, aside*): Oh... What is this dread I feel?... This terror...?

Ottavio (*to Géméa, menacingly*): I'm warning you! For the last time, vile wretch!... (*Drawing his dagger*) My patience is at an end! I'll not answer for my wrath!

Géméa: Then strike me dead, Ottavio!... (*With a grand gesture*) My blood will be on all your hands!... All you who remain silent... All you who hide the truth!...

Ottavio (*hesitating*): Then... (*Raising the dagger*) Then die!

(*As he is about to strike, Paola steps between them.*)

Paola: No!... (*With an anguished cry*) She... She could be my mother!

Ottavio: What?

Bianca (*to Paola*): Your...

Paola (*confused*): I... I don't know what I'm saying... I... (*To Bianca*) Oh, how you must have suffered!... But... But I am your daughter!... You are my mother!... You are!... Tell me that you are!...

Géméa (*to Bianca, coldly*): Yes! Tell her!... Here, in front of me, signora!... Tell her, why don't you!

Bianca (*pathetically*): My God!... My God!...

Paola (*despairing, taking Bianca in her arms*): Look!... See my tears!... They wait for your answer!... Tell me! I beg you... (*As Bianca, downcast, remains silent*) Oh! Why will you not speak?... What is this silence, that rejects me, disowns me...? What?... Have you taught me to love you... Have you filled my very soul with your image... fashioned my heart with love and devotion... joined my life to yours, my breath to your breath, only to reject me?... No, no!... I'll not believe it...

Géméa (*aside*):   Ah! How she loves her!

Paola (*growing more and more impassioned*):   I'll not, do you hear? (*Embracing her*) Do my arms not tell you that I am your daughter?... That I know in my heart that you are my mother?... What?... Am I not the child that you nurtured and raised?... I am! I am!... It is you who gave me my life!... Who give me my life!... Oh! Look at me!... Kiss me!

Bianca (*embracing her*):   My child!... Oh, my child!...

Géméa (*to Bianca*):   Swear that she is your daughter!... Why do you keep her waiting?

Bianca (*to Géméa*):   You... (*Aside*) That monster...

Ottavio (*to Bianca*):   Please, swear it, signora!... Let us all hear you!... You must! In the name of heaven... Please! You must!

Bianca (*aside*):   Ah, woe! Woe is me!

Paola (*to Bianca*):   Lie if you have to!... Say anything, I beg you! But do not reject me!... Nothing in the world will tear me from your arms, or rip you from my heart!

(*She falls weeping at Bianca's feet.*)

Bianca (*bending down, embracing her*):   Oh, Paola!... My daughter!...

Géméa (*to Bianca*):   Yes, signora... Duchess of the House of Lomellini!... Raise up your hands... Your blaspheming hands... (*Point-*

ing to the crucifix on the wall behind the shrine) And swear before your God!

Bianca (standing up, weakly): I... I will...

(She stands looking at the crucifix, hesitating.)

Géméa: Well?

Bianca (aside): God forgive me...

(She takes a few determined steps toward the shrine, and stops just as she is about to raise her hand.)

Paola (her hands joined together): Mother... Please...

(She takes her head in her hands. There is a moment of silence.)

Bianca (to Paola, pointing to Géméa, softly): She... She is your mother!

Paola (with a gasp): Oh!...

Ottavio (looking at Paola, aside): A... A Jewess!

(Ruccioni enters.)

SCENE 9
Géméa, Bianca, Paola, Ottavio, Ruccioni

Géméa (to Paola): You see, my child?... *(With a touch of sarcasm)* You need not wait until tomorrow... Come...

(Ruccioni stops short, in surprise.)

Paola (to Géméa): If... If only I might embrace her... Give one last kiss to the only mother I ever knew...

(*Géméa gestures her assent.*)

Paola (*to Bianca, pathetically*):   Nevermore may I call you my mother. But that name will always be yours in my heart!...

Bianca: Paola... My child...

(*They embrace, tearfully, as Ruccioni looks on, shaking his head in disbelief.*)

Paola: Farewell!... (*To Ottavio, passing before him*) Your poor betrothed must leave you, my darling...

Ottavio (*almost speechless*):   Paola...

Paola: Farewell!... (*To Géméa*) I am ready now... (*Weakly*) Mother...

Géméa (*aside*):   Ah! But no embrace... No kiss...

(*She takes her by the hand and leads her to the doorway. Paola offers no resistance, but, at the threshold, she stops, turns, and blows a wistful kiss to Bianca, as she and Géméa exit.*)

Bianca (*collapsing onto a chair*):   Will I ever see her again?... (*Looking heavenward*) Will I, dear God?

Ruccioni: Hope... Hope, signora...

CURTAIN

Act 4

A sumptuously furnished, semicircular hall in the Villa Negroni. Down right and left, corridors leading off. In the rear wall, two large, full-length double windows, heavily draped. Around the room, chairs, standing pedestals, statuary, etc. Center, a table.

At rise, liveried footmen are coming and going. Some are placing bouquets of flowers on the pedestals; others are laying bronze goblets on the table. Upstage, in front of the window, left, The Decorator is standing on a ladder, putting the finishing touches on the drapes, whose weighty mass Catarina, at the base of the ladder, is holding in her arms.

SCENE I
Catarina, The Decorator, Frigolini

The Decorator (*hammering the last few tacks, to Catarina*):   Say what you want, she must find it strange...

Catarina: The signorina...?

The Decorator (*nodding*):   Very strange...

(*He continues hammering.*)

Catarina: I should think so!... After living all these years with royalty!

The Decorator (*with a sweeping gesture*):   So instead, she gets herself a palace of her own!... (*With a sigh of admiration*) Say what you want... I still think so... (*Hammering*) And you, signora?... How long have you been working here?

Catarina: Me?... Three days...

The Decorator (hammering and nodding):   Aha...

Catarina: Thanks to her... Signorina Paola...

(*Frigolini, obviously very busy, enters quickly from the corridor, down left, overhearing the end of their exchange.*)

Frigolini: Hurry up, you two!... More work and less conversation!... Signora Géméa will be here any minute...

Catarina (with a little curtsy):   Very good, signore...

Frigolini: And she wants her surprise to be ready... Come, come...

Catarina: And what a surprise!... The Villa Negroni!... Wouldn't I love to find that in a birthday bouquet!

Frigolini (drawing aside one of the drapes on the window, right, looking out):   Ah!... What a view!... Magnificent...

Catarina: I should hope so! The whole gulf, spread out before your eyes...

(*Several Workmen enter, down left, carrying a chest and a number of large paintings.*)

Frigolini (to The Workmen):   You!... (*Pointing up right*) The chest, over there... And the two Titians, and the Raphael, in Signorina Paola's apartment... Come, I'll show you...

(*The Workmen follow him off, down right, as The Decorator finishes his work.*)

SCENE 2
The Decorator, Catarina

The Decorator (to Catarina):   There!... Now let it down gently... (*As she arranges the final drape)* No, say what you want... I pity her mother...

Catarina: Géméa?

The Decorator: I really do... She worships the ground her daughter walks on... But... (*With a shrug*) No use... The child has been sick since the moment she came to live with her...

Catarina: Sick...? Not really...

The Decorator (as he assembles his tools): Well, sad, then... Or home-sick... And that's even worse!... Damn! Say what you want, but people can die of it!

Catarina: They can?

The Decorator: Sometimes...

(*He climbs down.*)

Catarina: And the old woman knows, but there's nothing she can do... She does her best, but the past is always there, standing between them...

The Decorator (shaking his head): Poor thing!

Catarina: Just the other day, she was saying to me: "You ask me why I always weep when my daughter is praying?... It's because she's not praying to my God, but to another's..."

The Decorator (nodding): Ah...

Catarina: Well, if she's jealous of God himself, what do you expect!

(*Frigolini enters, down right.*)

Frigolini (to The Decorator): So... Finished?

The Decorator: Finished!

(He takes his ladder and, with a nod at Catarina, exits, down left.)

Frigolini (pointing down the corridor, left, to Catarina): Signora Géméa and her daughter will be coming in that way... Go stand in the carriage-drive and let me know the minute you see them.

Catarina (with an exaggerated little curtsy): Right away, signore... *(She begins to leave, down left, but returns.)* Oh... I almost forgot... Your... *(Handing him a key)* Your Majordomoship's gate-key...

Frigolini (pocketing it): Thank you.

(As Catarina exits, down left, Ruccioni enters, down right, unseen by Frigolini.)

SCENE 3
Frigolini, Ruccioni

Frigolini (beaming): "Your Majordomoship..." Ah!... And to think, me, Frigolini!... I thank heaven every day that I didn't throw in my lot with those thieves!... And with all that gold, staring me in the face... Me, a majordomo!... *(Reflecting)* Of course, there are thieves and there are... *(Finishing his thought with a gesture around the room)* But still, this way is better!

Ruccioni (behind him, tapping him on the shoulder): You think so?

Frigolini (turning, startled): You!... But...

Ruccioni: Shhh!... Not a word, or I'll strangle you! Understand?

Frigolini (scornfully): Same old Ruccioni!... What on earth are you doing here?

Ruccioni (*avoiding the question*):   Where is Paola?

Frigolini: Please, my friend... I'm an honest man these days...

Ruccioni: Only these days?... Ha!... You're much too modest!... And
besides, so am I an honest man... (*Emphasizing*) These days...

Frigolini: You are?... (*Embracing him*) Well, how nice to hear... (*After
patting him here and there, aside*) Not armed, at least... (*Aloud, rather
insolently*) Now then, my dear Signor Ruccioni...

Ruccioni: Shhh!

Frigolini: If I may say... (*Self-importantly*) As Signora Géméa's
majordomo... (*Holding up his thumb*) First: you did your best to
lead me astray!...

Ruccioni: Tsk tsk tsk!

Frigolini (*continuing, holding up his thumb and index finger*):   And
second: you punched me in the jaw and made off with Signora
Lomellini, when I was supposed to be guarding her!... I'm afraid
we have nothing to discuss!... (*Pointing right*) So... Kindly leave,
before I call the guards!

Ruccioni (*nodding, holding up his thumb and two fingers*):   Third!
Right?... Yes, well... (*Holding up his thumb*) First: you're a fool!...
(*Holding up his thumb and index finger*) Second: you just felt every inch of my body to see if I was armed, and you thought I didn't
notice!... Now... (*Pointing*) There's a terrace behind those drapes,
and it looks out over the water!... So... (*Holding up his thumb and
two fingers*) Third: one word or one false move, and I'll happily
drown Géméa's majordomo!... Is that clear?

Frigolini: If you're here to try and make off with Signorina Paola...

Ruccioni: I'm here because this is her birthday, and I promised the duchess that she would give her a kiss!... And you, my friend, are going to help me keep my promise!

Frigolini: Me?

Ruccioni: And it won't cost you a thin piaster, as Frimagusta would say!... So... You're going to tell Paola, or have someone tell her, that Signora Lomellini will be waiting for her by the gate, at the end of the carriage-drive... But first you'll give me the key...

Frigolini: I beg your pardon!

Ruccioni: If Signora Géméa, as you call her... (*Gesturing at the sumptuousness of the room*) If she can give her daughter such a magnificent birthday bouquet... A whole palace, I'll be damned!... Well, the kind soul who brought her up should be able to give her at least a flower, don't you think?

Frigolini: You... You're out of your mind! All the duchess wants to do is to... (*Trying to find a dignified word*)... to subvert her affection!

Ruccioni: "Subvert..." (*Pretending to be impressed*) My, my, my!... Now there's a big word for a runt of a man!

Frigolini (furious): "Runt"?... Who do you think... I'll have you know—

Ruccioni (interrupting): Besides, signore... When a fool of a major-domo wants to shut the gate up tight, he's even more of a fool when he wears big, open pockets...

(*He pulls the key from Frigolini's pocket and holds it up.*)

Frigolini: Give me that!

Ruccioni: Now, now!... (*Pocketing the key*) For the moment, all I need

from you is your silence! One word... Even a whisper, my friend...
And believe me, I'll hear you!

Frigolini: You... You're asking for trouble!

Ruccioni: Perhaps... But you're the one who'll get it!... (*Turning to leave, down right, sarcastically*) Until we meet again...

Frigolini (*shouting*):   Help!... Help!...

Ruccioni (*returning to him, thrusting his cap under his nose*):   Before you do that again, best have a look at this!

(*He shows him a stiletto piercing the crown of his cap.*)

Frigolini (*drawing back, terrified*):   A stiletto!

Ruccioni: Quite!... No longer than my finger, but it can kill a man before he can cry "help" a third time!... Even a majordomo!

Frigolini (*aside*):   My God!

Ruccioni: So, what do you say to that?

Frigolini (*under his breath*):   You scoundrel!

Ruccioni: Nothing?... Good!... (*He turns again to leave, down right.*)
Just as I thought... (*With a mock-serious little bow*) Once again, signore... (*Aside*) Ah! Another good deed!... When my collection is complete, I can go visit God without a worry in the world!

(*He exits.*)

Frigolini (*fuming*):   Oh!... The wretch!... The blackguard!...

(*Catarina comes running in, down left.*)

SCENE 4
Frigolini, Catarina

Catarina: They're coming!... They're coming!...

Frigolini: Quick!... You remember what you're to do?

Catarina: To the letter!

Frigolini: Good!

(*He waves her off and she exits, down right.*)

Frigolini (*looking about to make sure that everything is in order, then peering down the corridor, left*):   Ah!... Not a minute too soon...

(*Géméa enters, down left, walking backwards and leading Paola with one hand, and covering the latter's eyes with the other.*)

SCENE 5
Géméa, Paola, Frigolini

Géméa (*to Paola*):   No, no... You mustn't look...

Paola: Where are you taking me?

Géméa: You'll see...

Paola (*clinging to her, with a little laugh*):   Is this a game?

Géméa: Don't worry... I'll not let you fall...

Paola: What a child you are!

Géméa: Thanks to you, my darling...

Frigolini (watching them, aside):   Anything to amuse her... Poor thing!

(Shaking his head, he slips behind the drapes.)

Paola: Am I there yet?

Géméa: One more step...

Paola: Now?

Géméa: Now!... Turn around!... (*She takes her hand away from Paola's eyes and gives a loud clap.*) There!

(The drapes open, one after the other, and reveal a magnificent terrace covered with flowers, and birds in gilded cages. In the background, the waters of the Gulf of Genova, in bright sunlight, with its waves heard lapping against the foot of the terrace.)

Paola (turning, awestruck at the sight):   Oh!... It's... It's beautiful!... It's... Oh!... But... Where am I?

Géméa: At home... *Your* home...

Paola: This... This palace?

Géméa: Happy birthday, my child!

Paola: Oh!... Mother dearest!... What can I say...? (*She steps out onto the terrace, walking about, inspecting here and there.*) All these magnolias!... My favorite flower!... And these wonderful birds... And... (*Coming back inside, to Géméa*) Oh! Let me kiss you!

(She throws her arms around Géméa's neck and gives her a kiss.)

Géméa (as Paola, looks about the room, aside):   Ah! No greater reward...

Paola (*admiringly*):   What lovely things!... What elegant taste!... How did you ever... (*Stopping at the windows, looking out at the sea, suddenly recognizing something*) Oh!... Wait... I... I know this place!...

Géméa (*with a little shudder*):   You do?

Paola: It's the Gulf of Genova... That horizon... Those hills... And... And this must be the Villa Negroni!

Géméa: You know it?

Paola (*continuing, ignoring her question*):   Yes... It is! It is!... I remember now... Twelve years ago... We were returning from Taberca, and we sailed up to this very terrace!

Géméa: Ah...

Paola (*joyously*):   I was only a child... But what wonderful years!... (*At the terrace, pointing right, into the distance*) The lighthouse must be there... Off in the distance... Yes! It is!... I see it!... (*Looking in the other direction*) And on that side, a big cliff... (*Pointing*) There!... Off by the mountains!...

Géméa (*aside*):   Memories...

Paola (*gazing off the terrace, musing*):   And there!... That path... And that bench... Oh, yes! I remember...

Géméa (*aside*):   Memories I can never share...

Paola (*continuing*):   It was my birthday... Like today... And... And the others had been whispering, and giving each other little side-long looks... Then they left me there, all by myself... But, "I'll fool them," I thought, proud creature that I was... "I'll show them I'm not afraid to be alone!..." And I lay out on the bench...

(*Pointing*) That very one... With my arms for a pillow, humming a little tune... (*Reflecting*) *The Fishermen's Carol*... (*Nodding*) Of course!...

Géméa (*dejected, aside*):   A Christmas song...

Paola (*continuing*):   That wonderful, sweet melody that I can never forget... That comes back to me with my every memory... Or that brings them back to life, rising up like flocks of birds!... How well I remember! The sky was clear, the sea lay sleeping... The gentle breeze was rustling the grass, and bringing me fragrances I had never smelled before... I fell asleep and... Of all things, my singing seemed to go on through my slumber... But not in my own voice... It was so strange... Like a chorus of distant echoes... Far off, but suddenly coming nearer and nearer... So close that, when I opened my eyes, what did I see before me but a beautiful gondola, all decked out against the clear blue sky! And from it, like waves gently rolling in, that lovely melody, casting its spell... That... (*She stops suddenly, surprised.*) That... (*Listening*) Oh!... Listen!

(*In the distance can be heard a chorus of voices singing* The Fishermen's Carol, *and gradually approaching.*)

Géméa (*aside*):   That song...

Paola (*overjoyed*):   It is!... It's *The Fishermen's Carol!*... Oh! I can't believe it! It's just as I said...

Géméa (*aside*):   And coming closer...

Paola (*looking in the direction of the voices*):   And... And the gondola!... Look!... All decorated... The same as back then!

Géméa (*to Paola*):   For your birthday?

Paola (*replying*):   Yes... Oh, yes!

Géméa: And who was in it? Do you remember?

Paola: In the gondola?... I... (*Not wanting to answer*) No... I don't
remember...

(*A gondola can be seen passing a short distance off the terrace, with musi-
cians singing, and with Bianca, visible, standing at the prow.*)

Géméa (*pointing to it*):   Look there... Perhaps that will remind you...

Paola: Oh!... (*Aside*) My... (*Catching herself*) The duchess!

Géméa: Well?

Paola (*aside*):   Her!

Géméa: Did it?

Paola (*hesitating*):   I... I could barely see...

(*The gondola gradually disappears.*)

Géméa (*aside*):   Lies!... She saw, and she knew!

Paola (*following the gondola with her eyes*):   And off it goes... (*As the
singing grows silent*) No sound now but the wind... My song...
Gone now... Gone...

(*She remains at the window, absorbed in thought.*)

Géméa (*angrily, aside*):   Oh! That woman!... What? Not let a mother
enjoy her child in peace?... Seventeen years without her, and still
she begrudges me every minute by her side! (*Sighing, as she looks
at Paola, still musing by the terrace*) Ah... What more can I do to
make her forget? After all this... What else? What else? (*Struck

by an idea) Ah!... (*Calling*) Catarina!... (*Aside*) The way to every young lady's heart...

(*Catarina enters, down left.*)

SCENE 6
Géméa, Paola, Catarina

Catarina: Signora?

Géméa (*pointing to the chest, up right*):   In there... A jewel box... Bring it here!

(*Catarina complies.*)

Géméa (*taking out a pearl necklace, holding it up, to Paola*):   Look, my child!

Paola (*joining her*):   Oh!... How beautiful...!

Géméa (*taking out other jewels*):   And these...? (*Going to the chest and taking out a lace shawl, as Paola watches, agog with admiration*) And this...?

Paola: My goodness!... I never...

Catarina: Oh!... Fit for a princess!

Géméa (*to Paola*):   All yours, my darling...

Paola (*almost speechless*):   I... I don't know what...

Géméa (*to Paola, putting the shawl on her head*):   Here... See how lovely... (*To Catarina*) The pins, Catarina... (*To Paola*) Just a moment... (*To Catarina, pointing to the chest.*) The ones with the rubies... (*To Paola*) Almost done... Then you'll see...

(*Catarina goes to the chest and takes out the pins.*)

Catarina (*to Géméa*):   These, signora?

Géméa: Ah!... (*Taking them and arranging them on the shawl*) Perfect!... Perfect!...

Paola (*to Géméa*):   But... Such elegant things!... Where ever did you get such exquisite taste... Down to the last detail!... I never...

Géméa (*continuing the arrangement, beaming*):   Where?... From the most important source of all... (*As Paola fidgets a bit*) No, no... Stay still... Almost done... (*Replying*) From the heart, my child!... (*Finishing*) There!... (*Handing her a mirror, jovially*) Has your lady-in-waiting been equal to the task? Are you satisfied with her?

Paola (*giving her back the mirror*):   Oh, yes!

Géméa (*a little pathetically*):   And... you are happy?

Paola (*clapping her hands*):   I am! I am!...

(*As she is about to throw her arms around Géméa's neck, the singing can be heard again, faintly, and she stops short.*)

Paola: Oh... (*Going to the terrace, as if in a dream*) Listen...

Géméa (*aside*):   Again?... (*To Paola*) My child...

Paola (*ignoring her, in a whisper*):   She's going to pass by...

Géméa (*aside*):   And me?... Do I exist...

Paola (*in a whisper*):   And I'll see her again...

Géméa (*aside*):   Does she know?... Does she care?...

Paola (*blowing a kiss in the direction of the approaching gondola, sadly, aside*):   Sweet breeze, take this kiss to the one who was once my mother!

(*As she listens, the gondola reappears, farther offshore than before, and gradually disappears.*)

Géméa: Ah, no... (*Shaking her head, sadly*) No... No...

Paola (*as the sounds of the singing die away*):   No more... No more...

Géméa (*aside*):   God help me!

(*She breaks into tears and exits, down left.*)

Paola (*rousing herself from her musings, to Catarina*):   Did my mother leave?

Catarina: Yes, signorina...

Paola (*coming downstage*):   Oh, my!... I'm afraid I've made her sad again, in spite of myself!... All about me, nothing but regrets, and sighs, and tears... Two mothers, two woes... If only I could erase that past that tortures the one, or die of that future that torments the other!... Am I to blame if each has her place in my heart?

Catarina: Signorina...

Paola: One, for my memories, and the other, for my respect... (*Wringing her hands*) How... How can I go on?... This dilemma will be the death of me...

Catarina: Please...

Paola: It will! It will!... Ah! If only I could keep them both by my side... Each one, my mother! Me, a daughter to each!... How tenderly I would press them to my breast!... But no!... God above stands between them!... God, and our life itself... (*She collapses onto an armchair.*) My God!... My God!...

Catarina (*trying to cheer her*):   Oh, signorina!... How that shawl becomes you!... Why, you look the very image of a madonna!... Or a beautiful young bride...

Paola (*quickly standing up*):   A bride? (*Moving down right, distraught, to herself*) Me, a bride?... Me, betrothed to grief?... Betrothed to death?... Can they not see that my life ebbs away?... Ah! Enough, you vain promise of happiness! Enough!... (*Ripping off the shawl*) My brow needs no icy folds of lace to remind it of my mourning! (*As if addressing the shawl*) Leave me alone!... (*Flinging it to the floor*) Leave me to my despair!

(*She exits, down right.*)

Catarina (*shaking her head*):   Poor dear! (*She picks up the shawl and returns it to the chest, looking right, into the wings, ostensibly at Paola*) See how she stands there, not knowing what to do...

(*Géméa enters, down left.*)

Géméa: Ah!... Now my house is full, but how empty is my heart! (*To Catarina, noticing her.*) Please!... I want to be alone...

Catarina: Yes, signora... (*Aside*) Poor thing!

(*She exits, down right.*)

SCENE 7
Géméa, alone

Géméa: This struggle will kill me!... This battle against the past... Already I hear all my illusions crumbling, all my hopes dashed to bits. Would it not be better to pull down the last stone, let it crush me, once and for all!... Ah, yes... She would choose her... That woman over me... And that would be the end of it! Nothing to be done... The very thought draws me to it, like a gaping abyss. It burns my brain, it gnaws at my heart... (*She staggers for a moment, clutching her head.*) No need to go on... No reason to live... (*Looking about*) Where is she now, I wonder... (*Looking offstage, down right, to where Paola has ostensibly been standing since her exit*) Ah! There... All alone, her head in her hands... Thinking... But of whom? (*Bitterly*) Yes, that's the question!... (*Sighing*) Oh! If only I could love her less!... And why not?... Good God, what if I tried?... Where is it written that this sacred passion, this blessèd mother's love, should be so filled with the jealousy of a frenzied, fevered soul?... Ah, but whose fault...? Not mine, but my misfortune's!... Jealous? Yes, I am!... Jealous of that past, where I have no part... Jealous of that woman, who challenges me for her thoughts... Jealous of Ottavio, whom another chose for her to wed... Jealous of her God!... Yes, jealous of Him, because He casts me from her heart!... Oh! If only... If only...

(*As she paces back and forth, Bianca enters, down left, unseen by her.*)

Géméa (*continuing, in deep despair*):   No! It cannot go on!... It must end!... Oh, yes! It must end... And it shall!

Bianca (*overhearing, to Géméa, approaching behind her*):   With her death?

SCENE 8
Géméa, Bianca

Géméa (*turning*):   You!

Bianca (*pointing offstage, toward where Paola is standing*):   With that poor child's death?... Is that how it will end?

Géméa: You?... Here?... I should have known!... My tears should have told me!

Bianca: Géméa...

Géméa: So, once again... You and I, together... The Christian and the Jewess... You, heir to seventeen centuries of oppression against my people... And I, heir to as many centuries of woe, and wrath, and curses against yours!... Look at us!... You, worse still, because you keep me from my child!... You, who stole my daughter, and gave me back a stranger!...

Bianca: Géméa...

Géméa: But you have done still more!... You told her: "That race..." (*Emphasizing*) *Her* race, signora!... "That race is vile, yet it treats us as vile!... It is hateful, and yet it is ours that it despises!..." Yes, you excused in her eyes all your bloodthirsty Christian crimes against us... So often and so well that, in her vision of the past, with its generations of pathetic voices weeping and wailing the desperate agony of her race... (*Emphasizing again*) *Her* race, signora... Ah! So well that she too must have clapped her hands in glee at the crumbling House of Jacob... She too must have fanned the flames of the stakes where her ancestors were burned alive, must have trampled the bones and the ashes of her fathers, with never a notion of the crimes she was committing against her people!... That, signora... That is what you have done to my child!... Adultery can be forgiven... And theft, even murder... But this sacrilege? Never!... And if God were to forgive it... Any God, even mine!... If He were to cleanse a soul of this murderous sin, then I would cast Him from my heart, reject Him, and raise my hands to heaven to damn His very name!

Bianca: Your curses do not surprise me, Géméa... But... (*Pointing offstage, right*) She is the reason for my presence... She alone...

Géméa: My child?

Bianca: Your... (*Hesitating*) Yes, your child.

Géméa (growing more and more angry):   Can you not understand? Will you never—

Bianca (interrupting her, calmly):   Please... Look at her first, before you go on...

Géméa: Look at her?... (*With a shudder of apprehension*) Why?

Bianca: Can you not see how pale she is?

Géméa: Pale?... (*Looking toward Paola*) My daughter?

Bianca: Pale as death, Géméa...

Géméa: Are you saying that she is ill?

Bianca: Must you ask? Is it not plain?

Géméa: My child?... Ill...? (*Looking toward Paola*) Yes... Pale... How deathly pale... Good God! I should have seen... (*To Bianca*) What is it? What illness?

Bianca: Think...

Géméa: All I saw was my own grief... (*To Bianca*) But what is it? Tell me... You brought her up... You know her better than I! What can it be?

Bianca: Think...

Géméa (after a weighty pause, softly):   Ah, yes... I understand...

(*She sits down.*)

Bianca: When I adopted Paola I had only one thought... To do a good deed... Nothing else mattered! How could I think of the harm I might be doing?... The consequences of my act...? Now the harm is done, and I am sorry, Géméa... Truly, truly sorry...

Géméa (*with a sardonic little nod*):   Sorry... No doubt...

Bianca: I beg you to forgive me!... If only you could... You suffer, but so do I... You weep, and I weep with you!

Géméa (*sarcastically*):   Ah! She weeps!... Not even can I shed my tears in peace!

Bianca: One look at Paola... One single glance, and such pain gripped my heart!... That pallor bodes her no good, believe me!... She languishes, withers like a poor wilting flower, suddenly plucked and transplanted to another soil.

Géméa (*looking offstage, toward Paola*):   So pale... So weak...

Bianca: But she can be cured... Brought back to life...

Géméa: Ah...

Bianca: *We* can cure her, Géméa!

Géméa: She is as you have made her...

Bianca (*ignoring her remark*):   I am leaving for the country. Two months in my villa... Not one day more... (*Géméa gives her a quizzical look.*) If... If only you will do what I ask of you... For her!...

Géméa: Do...?

Bianca: I beg you!... I... I swear before God that, if you let me take her with me, I shall bring her back to you... I swear it!

Géméa: Ha!... Let you take her with you...? Is it going to be easier for her to forget you once you nurse her back to health?... Come,

come!... Let us be frank!... This is merely a new duel!... I fought to save her from the past. Now death is the enemy, and I shall fight no less to save her once again!

Bianca: And you dare pretend to love her?

Géméa: Pretend...? (*Wringing her hands*) My God! My God!... How much more can I love her?... I can never give her up! And I never will!... But listen to me... Hear what I have to say... If she leaves, she leaves... So be it...

Bianca: What do you mean?

Géméa: That either she stays, and remains my child forever... Or she leaves, and I never lay eyes on her again!

Bianca: But...

Géméa: I'll not go on living in your shadow! I'll not have you prowling about, spying to see how pale she grows!... It's time we drop our masks, you and I!... I hate you! What more need I say?... For seventeen endless years this duel of ours has lasted!... Now it must end... And in the clear light of day! Once and for all, we shall see which one of us is loved the more!

Bianca: Take care, Géméa...

Géméa: Enough of this torment!... Not knowing, from moment to moment, if one is truly loved or not!... Call her... The choice will be hers... You or me!

Bianca: The choice...?

Géméa: Between her mother and a stranger!

Bianca: A stranger...? Say, rather, between the one who conceived her, and the one who loved and raised her...

Géméa: Hers alone will be the choice! (*Apostrophizing*) O child's tender love!... We shall see if you are merely vain words!... And you, O nature!... Nothing but a lie!... (*To Bianca*) Let her come!...

Bianca: Again, take care, Géméa... My rights will speak for themselves!

Géméa: But mine are sacred!

Bianca: My love is boundless!

Géméa: And mine is holy!

Bianca: I shall call on the eloquence and influence of her past!

Géméa: Nature will plead my cause for me!... (*Calling*) Paola!... (*To Bianca*) Nature, and my God!... (*Calling*) Paola!... Paola!... (*To Bianca*) My God, and nature!

(*Paola enters, down right, without noticing Bianca.*)

SCENE 9
Géméa, Bianca, Paola

Paola: Mother dearest...?

Géméa (*pointing to Bianca*): Which one?

Paola: Which... (*Noticing her, aside*) God help me!

Bianca (*to Paola*): Yes... Here you are, between us both... Both your mothers!

Géméa (*to Paola*): One too many... Your heart has room for but one. It is time you choose!

Paola (*aside*): Choose?... (*Aloud*) But...

Bianca (pointing to Géméa):   She is your mother! But I am your mother too!... She gave birth to your flesh, but I gave birth to your soul!... It was I who gave you that Christian faith, and the salvation that it alone bestows!... You were not more than two years old when I took you... It was at the Convent of the Annunciation... The great organ was playing... The mother superior was weeping as she blessed us... At that very moment I felt that you were a part of me, and that I was a part of you. And I cried out: "What a miracle that God has joined two souls together!... That He gives to me, a stranger, a mother's heart to love this child... This angel, dear God, that you entrust to me... That I shall turn into a saint, so that, one day, when the time comes to return to your bosom, all the more glorious will she be!..." Then I picked you up in my arms, and bore you off... And that is how I became your mother, and how you became my child.

Géméa (to Paola):   I did nothing for you... How could I? That joy was taken from me!... I did no more than bring you into the world and give you life! And oh, what a dreadful life it was! Poverty all about us... My friends, pale and sickly... The doctor, shuddering that something terrible was going to happen... Your poor father, without work... "It's in the stars," I whispered to the doctor, "someone is going to die!" "Old wives' tales!" he muttered, and he drew back, afraid... "Yes, someone is going to die," I repeated, "but save my child, whatever you do!" This time he gave no answer... "Save my child!" I cried, raising my voice still higher and higher. "Save my child! Save my child!..." And he did... You lived... Just so that, today, you might choose between myself and a stranger... Now, you decide!

Paola: Oh, God!

Bianca (to Paola):   How often does the life she bears cost a mother her own! But is death the greatest sacrifice? Sickly and frail, you needed all my attention, all the care I could give you. And so, young as I was, I forgot my own youth to devote myself to you. I watched you grow in my arms, and then in your cradle. And when the cradle became too small, I gave you my very bed, and would sleep at your feet if ever you were ill... There was nothing I would not do, no sacrifice I would not make... Nothing I would not take from my own life, to strengthen and nourish yours. You were living, and I was happy... Happy to watch you live!...

Géméa (*to Paola*):   And how many tears did her happiness cost me! A mother's love is unlike any other!... Look at her! She tells you: "Oh, how I have suffered!" Ah, but I ask you, can one suffer so much and still be so fair?... Has suffering dulled her beauty?... One age, we two... Yet I could be her mother! (*To Bianca, as she is about to object*) No, please! I must finish!... (*To Paola*) And she speaks of her devotion! (*Sarcastically*) What a relief to hear her!... But real mothers do not count up their tears, to glory in them anon. What is sacrifice for a stranger is happiness for us!... Ah! Are we not repaid with a babe's simple smile? And is that little life, growing day by day, not a joy to behold and a blessing on our house?... To watch a child grow... One's own... Ah, yes, you grew... But, alas, I was weeping... You babbled your first "mamma"... But I was weeping... You became a beautiful, lovely young lady... But I... I was weeping!... What could have... What should have been my pride was my agony! How often did I reach out into space, and cry: "My child! My child!" only to clutch with frantic arms at what was never there! How often did I beg the wind to carry to you the echo of my voice, the breath of my kiss!... I had wrapped myself about, buried myself in your memory, searching for you, yearning for you... Will you not, now, take pity on your mother?

Bianca (*to Paola*):   What? Would you be without pity for me?... Without pity for yourself?... It is no longer two women who struggle for your soul! It is truth against falsehood, Paola! Take care...

Paola (*taking her head in her hands*):   My God! My God!

Bianca (*pointing to Géméa*):   Choose her, and you betray your God!

Géméa (pointing to Bianca):   Choose her, and you renounce your people!

Paola (in utter despair):   Enough!... I beg of you...

Bianca: You are a Christian!

Géméa: You never were!

Bianca: But now you are!... God placed me on your path! He speaks to you in my voice!

Géméa: Lies!... Blasphemous lies!

Bianca: Look!... He stands there, in Judea, on the *Via Dolorosa*... He shows you His holy sacrifice... A God, willing to die for your eternal salvation!... He shows you his executioners, cursing Him, jeering at Him... Calvary's blood... The world, in torment... Jerusalem, in tears... You, a Christian... Would you live amongst His enemies?

Paola: Oh!

Géméa: Would you live amongst those who condemned your race ever to wander the face of the earth? Look at this people, scattered over the globe... It is our race! Mine and yours!... Borne off on the tide, on the waves of its own blood! Beset by fire, beset by the sword... Night's flames glow to betray it... Not an hour goes by but that gibbets rise up and men die, hanged... Not a day, but that old men, and women, and children blend their desperate cries as they burn at the stake!... The world knows, and it laughs... (*Paola listens, more and more intently, obviously moved.*) But even as the leaves fall, the tree stands fast and lives!... Men scorn, and despise, and curse them... They are herded together like packs of beasts... The very air they breathe has its price, and even life itself!

Paola: Oh!... But why...

Géméa (continuing):   Everything has been stripped from them...
Pillaged, ransacked... Even the hope of a land of their own...
Everything, but their God!

Bianca (to Paola):   No!... You must not listen!... You will be damned!

Géméa (continuing, as Paola ignores Bianca's pleading):   And that God
it is, who speaks to you now, who cries out in my voice: "Jewess
you are, and Jewess you must remain!... Your mother's God comes
first!... Come back to us!... Come, Noémi!... Come, daughter of
Ben-Meïr!... We have nothing to tempt you with but the woe we
have endured... But that woe is sacred! You too shall feel the scorn
heaped upon your mother... (*Paola begins sobbing.*) The tortures
that killed your father may, one day, kill you as well... But what
does it matter? We claim you as one more victim of their oppression. Would you suffer like your mother? Would you perish by her
side?..."

Paola (sobbing):   Oh...

Géméa (to Bianca, who is about to interrupt):   Ah, you!... Be still! Can
you not see that she is weeping?

Bianca: Paola!... My Paola...

Géméa (to Paola):   Weep your fill, my child! Your tears are good, for
I see that it is in joy that they are shed!

Paola: What is this feeling that I have never felt before?

Bianca: My child!

Paola (ignoring her):   A new feeling within me...

Géméa (*to Paola*):   Ah! I know in my heart that, at last, you have come back!

Paola: When I hear her voice, it is myself that I seem to hear...

Bianca: No!... My Paola!... No!...

Géméa (*to Paola, holding out her arms to her*):   Your mother is here, my darling!

Paola (*throwing herself into Géméa's embrace*):   Oh, mother! Mother dearest!... Take me!... Take me in your arms, and carry me off!... (*She gives her a kiss.*) Let me know how much you love me!

Géméa (*pressing her to her breast*):   Ah! At last, a kiss from the heart!... From the very soul!

Bianca (*to Paola*):   And so... Farewell!

Paola (*aside*):   How quickly I forget her... (*To Bianca*) Already, signora?

Bianca: Already... And forever!

Paola: Not so much as... Not even a kiss...?

Bianca: No!

Géméa (*to Paola*):   Come... Come...

Paola: Ah!... My God!... (*Looking at Géméa*) One bore me in her womb... (*Looking at Bianca*) One chose me, gave me my life... (*She stands, bewildered, clutching her head.*) Oh! My head... My head... (*To Bianca, weakly, as if to explain herself*) She... She is my mother, signora... Please... Please forgive me...

Bianca (*coldly*): You have renounced your God!

(*Paola stands, distraught and visibly shaken.*)

Géméa (*to Paola*): Come...

Paola (*without hearing her*): Oh... My soul...

Géméa: Come, my child...

Paola: Damned!... Damned forever!

Géméa: We must be gone...

Paola (*confused*): Gone...? Where...? Is this not my home? Should I not be here? (*Clutching her head*) Oh! My head... My... (*To both of them*) Every word you speak kills me! Why can you not see it?... Does your love give you the right to torment my sick heart?... You would have me choose to reject my God or to betray my mother!... How can I?... How?... (*To Géméa*) When you have torn from me the altars of my faith, what then will I be? (*To Bianca*) When you have made me curse and revile my mother, how will that profit you?... Ah, woe! Woe is me...

Géméa: My child...

Bianca: Paola...

Paola (*to Géméa*): No!... It is not your child that you love... (*To Bianca*) It is not your Paola... (*To both of them*) It is yourselves that you love, in me!... No one but yourselves!... (*To Géméa*) You have built my despair, stone by stone, with your hopes... (*To Bianca*)... and laid on me the curse of my damnation with your faith!... (*To both of them*) You, loving hearts?... Ah, no! Deadly souls!... You, loving mothers?... Ah, no! Not at all!... And, it is I, your daughter... Alas, I who must accuse you!... No!... If one cannot have me, then neither shall the other! I reject you both!... (*Pressing her hands to her bosom)* You, heartless mothers!... Out of my sight, selfish creatures!... Out of my sight!...

Géméa: My child...

Bianca: My love...

Paola: Oh! I... I am dying... (*Clutching her head*) Ah... (*Pushing Géméa and Bianca away as each tries to approach her*) Let the dead die in peace!... (*Beginning to rave*) Each one, pressed against my heart... Stifling my breath... Impossible to breathe... Ah! Leave me alone!... Out of my sight!... I beg you! Out of my sight!... I... (*Staggering*) Ah...

(*She falls to the ground in a swoon.*)

Géméa: My God!... I have killed her!... I have killed my Noémi...

(*Sobbing, she takes Paola in her arms, as Bianca, agape, stares at them, transfixed.*)

CURTAIN

Act 5

The Villa Negroni gardens, with trees, flowering paths, little hillocks here and there. Off in the distance, the church of San Lucco. Down left, beneath a tree, a bench. The entire stage right side is occupied by one of the façades of the villa, with a practicable covered balcony running its length, in the middle of which is a door leading inside, flanked by several arcades covered with vines and flowers. A short staircase leads up to the balcony.

At rise, it is a moonlit evening. Three Doctors, gravely walking back and forth, are conferring in the garden.

SCENE I
Frigolini, The Doctors

The Second Doctor (*categorically*):   But I'm absolutely certain...

Frigolini (*appearing on the balcony, aside*):   My, my!... All this time, and still consulting?... Not a good sign, I'm afraid... (*Coming down the stairs, to The Doctors*) Is there anything I can do for the dottori?

The First Doctor: No, my good man...

Frigolini (*aside*):   Tsk tsk tsk!... Poor signorina!

(*He exits left, through the garden, shaking his head.*)

The Second Doctor: But I...

The First Doctor (*ignoring him*):   This morning, another attack of delirium... But who can say? By tomorrow, perhaps complete dementia...

The Third Doctor (nodding sagely): If not sooner...

The Second Doctor: But...

The Third Doctor: You say her father died *non compos mentis?*

The First Doctor: Quite...

The Second Doctor: But opium is certainly indicated! How can you doubt it?

The First Doctor: With these symptoms?... Not wise... Not wise...

The Second Doctor (angrily): I assure you... How can you...

The Third Doctor (calming him down): My dear colleague! Please...

The First Doctor (to The Second Doctor): I do, however, agree with your recommendation that the patient be moved...

The Second Doctor (sarcastically): Thank you! I appreciate your confidence!

The First Doctor (continuing): Especially away from her mother... Perhaps by suppressing the causative element of the illness, we might suppress the illness itself. Peace and quiet will do more to effect a cure, in my opinion, than even the most skillful physician.

The Second Doctor: Oh? And who might that be, may I ask?

The First Doctor: What a question, from one of the leading lights of our profession!

The Second Doctor: You flatter me!

The First Doctor: Perhaps she could be put in the care of Signora Lomellini...

The Third Doctor: The duchess?

The First Doctor: Yes... She's a kind and gentle lady... Very even-tempered...

The Third Doctor: Excellent choice... I heartily concur...

The Second Doctor: But I still insist...

The First Doctor (ignoring him):   Let me go see if I can convince Signora Géméa to agree...

(*He goes up the staircase. As he goes inside, Frigolini returns, entering left.*)

SCENE 2
The Second Doctor, The Third Doctor, Frigolini

The Second Doctor (hailing Frigolini):   I say... You!...

Frigolini: Dottore?

The Second Doctor: My hat... My walking stick...

(*Frigolini nods, goes up the stairs, and goes inside. The two Doctors stand nodding at each other with a professional air.*)

The Second Doctor (after a moment or two):   Yes... Opium... No question...

The Third Doctor: Perhaps... But one must consider—

The Second Doctor (interrupting, holding out his snuff box):   A pinch of snuff, my friend?

The Third Doctor (taking a pinch):   Thank you... Too kind...

(*They both proceed to sniff.*)

The Second Doctor (*reverting to his idée fixe*):   In the proper dose, of
   course...

The Third Doctor (*confused*):   Of snuff?

The Second Doctor: Of... No!... Of opium, *perbacco!*... How many
   times—

The Third Doctor (*interrupting, pointing to the church in the
   distance*):   Ah, look!... The little church of San Lucco!... With its
   beautiful stained-glass windows all lit up...

The Second Doctor (*straining to see*):   Windows...? (*Squinting*) What
   good eyes you have!... (*Putting on his glasses, rather annoyed*) Even
   with my spectacles...

(*Frigolini appears at the door with the walking stick and hat, and comes
down the stairs.*)

The Third Doctor: Today is a feast day. It must be for evening prayers.

The Second Doctor (*taking off his glasses, wiping them vigorous-
   ly*):   Damnation! (*Putting them on again, squinting, aside*) Church?
   What church?

Frigolini (*to The Second Doctor*):   Dottore...

The Second Doctor (*angrily taking off his glasses and putting them away,
   to Frigolini, sharply*):   You!... Can't you see I'm busy?... Give me
   those!

(*He seizes the hat and walking stick, impatiently, from a somewhat bewildered Frigolini.*)

Frigolini: Dottore...?

The Second Doctor: Go... (*Frustrated*) Go fly a kite!

Frigolini (aside):   A kite...? Why on earth... (*Aloud, to The Second Doctor*) But I don't even own one... (*Aside*) He's out of his mind!

(*Bianca and Ottavio enter, left.*)

SCENE 3
Frigolini, The Second Doctor, The Third Doctor, Bianca, Ottavio

Frigolini (embarrassed to see Bianca, aside):   Her!... (*To Bianca*) I... I hope the duchess harbors no ill will... I mean... After the other night...

Bianca: Please go see if Géméa will receive us.

Frigolini (with an obsequious little bow):   Indeed...

(*He goes up the stairs and in the door.*)

The Second Doctor (to Bianca):   We were just mentioning your name, signora...

(*He and Bianca amble upstage, along the façade, chatting softly.*)

Ottavio (to The Third Doctor, anxiously):   How is she, dottore? Is there any improvement?

The Third Doctor: I fear her condition is much the same, my friend...

(*They too move off, up left, along one of the paths, continuing their conversation sotto voce, as Bianca and The Second Doctor return downstage.*)

Bianca (to The Second Doctor):   But Géméa will never agree!

The Second Doctor: But she must!... It's our only hope! (*Aside, under his breath*) Except for opium...

Bianca: Oh!

(*Frigolini and The First Doctor reappear and come down the stairs.*)

Frigolini (*to Bianca*):   Signora Géméa asks the duchess to be good enough to come back another time.

(*He gives a curt little bow, climbs the stairs, and exits.*)

Bianca (*to The Second Doctor*):   You see?

SCENE 4
The Three Doctors, Bianca, Ottavio

The Second Doctor (*to The First Doctor*):   Well?

The First Doctor: She refuses.

The Second Doctor: Perhaps she'll reconsider...

The First Doctor: I left a certain Signore Ruccioni with her. Something of a blusterer, but his devotion has been exemplary throughout this ordeal... He has taken it upon himself to attempt to persuade her.

Bianca: Ruccioni...?

The First Doctor: The signorina's godfather, it seems...

Bianca (*nodding*):   Yes...

The First Doctor: One would say that you are not all wholly blameless in this unhappy affair, signora.

Bianca (*with a deep sigh*):   No...

The First Doctor: You agree?

Bianca: I do... Yes, yes!... (*Beginning to weep*) But oh! How I have paid!... How terribly I have paid!

Ottavio (*coming downstage, apostrophising*):   O Paola!... My poor Paola!...

Bianca: Ottavio...

Ottavio (*continuing*):   If you died I would have joined you... Stayed by your side... Followed you in death...

Bianca: My friend...

(*Ruccioni appears on the balcony and comes down the stairs.*)

Ottavio (*continuing*):   But to see you, to speak to you, and know that you cannot hear me... Not know who I am... To feel you there, close to me, and know that your soul is so far, so far away... My God!... How can it be?

SCENE 5
The Three Doctors, Bianca, Ottavio, Ruccioni

The First Doctor (*to Ruccioni*):   So?

Ruccioni: Nothing, dottore...

The First Doctor: And her reasons?

Ruccioni: None...

Bianca (*to Ruccioni*):   And Paola...?

Ruccioni (*shaking his head*):   Ah! What a cruel curse is madness, signora! She watches her mother weep, and she laughs!... Poor child! It's not her fault... Laughing, weeping... It's all the same in her distress! In the loneliness of her folly!... Just now she dressed up all in white, like a bride! And she took my hand, and she said: "Quick, signore! Take me to the altar! Ottavio is waiting..."

Ottavio: Oh... (*Holding back his tears*) My Paola...

(*He moves left, distraught.*)

Ruccioni (*to Ottavio*):   Yes... Weep, count... Well you might... (*To Bianca, who has moved left, joining Ottavio, to console him*) Then, all of a sudden, she bends her head and leans forward, listening... "Oh! My soul has become a bird! Hear how prettily it sings!..." Next moment, she sees a light, from out in the garden... "No, no... It's a star... Oh! See how it shines!..." And she goes running off, like a gazelle, and crying: "My soul is flying away! I must catch it!... I must! I must!..."

Bianca: And Géméa?

Ruccioni (*approaching her, left*):   She shakes her head and goes after her, poor thing! Like a ghost clinging to the trail of a shadow!... So sad... So sad... The daughter's madness will soon be hers as well!

Bianca: Please, Signor Ruccioni...

Ruccioni: Ah, signora! How wrong we all were to do as we did back then!... All of us... Each and every one...

Bianca: Alas!

Ruccioni (*continuing*):   Signora Marta, for taking the child... Me, for helping them baptize her... You, for mothering her... God doesn't like His handiwork undone. It can only bring bad luck.

_____

(*He walks slowly across the garden, shaking his head, and exits, left.*)

Ottavio (*weakly*):   Paola... Paola...

Bianca (*taking his hand*):   My son...

(*As the two stand for a long moment, deep in their despair, the church bells of San Lucco, off in the distance, begin to chime. Paola, dressed in white, attracted by the sound, appears on the balcony with Géméa close behind her.*)

The First Doctor (*first to notice her, gesturing*):   Ah!... Look...

SCENE 6
The Three Doctors, Ottavio, Bianca, Géméa, Paola

Paola: Oh... (*As if in a dream*) The voices of heaven!... (*As she comes down the stairs, followed by Géméa*) Floating in the air, like my soul... Like Paola's poor soul... Weeping... Weeping...

Géméa: How much more...

Paola (*continuing*):   Why?... (*Clutching her head*) Oh! The pain... How it hurts poor Paola to think...

(*She crosses left and sits down on the bench, motionless and as if in a daze.*)

Géméa: Oh! How much more, dear God?

The First Doctor (*to Géméa, approaching her*):   Géméa...

Géméa: Please! Leave me alone! I beg you...

The First Doctor: Again, I must repeat... Only a miracle can save her now!

Géméa: A miracle?... (*After a moment, almost in a whisper, resigned*) Then take her!... No miracles will God perform for me!...

172

The First Doctor: Ah...

Géméa (weakly): No miracles, my friend...

The First Doctor: I knew that your heart would not let you—

Géméa (interrupting): But first... You must tell me, dottore... You, whom I trust... You, a man of honor...

The First Doctor: Yes...?

Géméa: Swear to me... Swear, on that sacred honor... (*Pointing to Bianca*) Swear that it was not her family that told you what to say!

The First Doctor: Signora! I am a man of science!... Surely you cannot believe that—

Géméa (interrupting): Please! Swear it, I beg of you!...

The First Doctor: Before God, and on my honor, I so swear!

Géméa (sighing): Then so be it... It is done... (*Bitterly*) If only a miracle can save her... A miracle... (*To The First Doctor*) Bring the duchess Lomellini to me... (*Aside, as he complies*) Her!... Oh, the bitter pill... Enough! Enough!... (*To Bianca, pointing to The First Doctor*) No doubt he has told you...

Bianca (taking her hand, sincerely): You poor, suffering soul!

(*Géméa pulls her hand away, sharply.*)

The First Doctor (to Géméa, almost in a whisper): Géméa...

Géméa (struggling to control her emotions, to Bianca): I entrust her to you, signora... (*Bianca bows her head.*) But as I do... As I do... (*Unable to continue*) Ah!... What more is there to say?... (*Pointing to Paola, still seated on the bench, left*) Take her!... Take her! And be quick!...

(*She turns aside, weeping, her head in her hands. As Bianca and Ottavio lead Paola right, the latter, noticing Géméa, stops short before her.*)

Paola (*pointing*): Oh, look!... That poor old woman... (*She goes over and gives Géméa an unemotional little embrace.*) Please, signora... Why do you weep?

Géméa (*pressing her to her bosom*): My child!... My child!... (*To The First Doctor*) How can I, dottore... How can I let her go?... My flesh... My blood...

(*She continues weeping bitterly.*)

Bianca (*to The First Doctor*): We must let her weep, my friend... Tears are God's gift. They give us the strength to make sacrifices in His name... Sacrifices we are too weak to perform without Him.

(*She and The First Doctor move up left, away from the pair, leaving them together. As Paola slowly breaks free from Géméa's embrace, Ottavio falls on his knees at her feet.*)

Ottavio (*pathetically*): Paola!... My belovèd... My betrothed... (*Tearfully*) My Paola!

(*She gives him a quizzical, uncomprehending look, picks a flower, and, fascinated by it, moves upstage, plucking its petals one by one, leaving Ottavio, head in hands, prostrate in his grief.*)

SCENE 7
Géméa, Paola

Géméa (*to Paola, following behind*): Speak to me, my child!... Ah! What more have I need to live? Why should I not die?... Why?... Tell me, my child!... Why?

Paola (*looking vaguely about*): "My child..."? Whose child?... Who

calls me her child? (*Taking Géméa's hand*) You, signora?... You?...
(*As Géméa covers her hand with kisses*) But... Why am I so alone, if
you say that you are my mother?

Géméa (*aside*):   God help me!

Paola (*up right*):   When I was ill, my mother would always pray...
When I... (*Clutching her head*) Oh!... The pain... The pain...

Géméa: My child...

Paola: But why do you not pray, signora, if you say you are my
mother?

Géméa: I have prayed, but God is deaf to my voice...

Paola (*looking at her, naively*):   Ah! But you must make yourself very
small to pray... When we pray, we must be humble, signora.

Géméa (*coming down right*):   For seventeen years, I joined my hands
in prayer and raised them to heaven!... Seventeen endless years...
And today, too, I prayed... But see? They take you from me!... How
could you know?... Yes, again they take you from me, rip you from
my arms... (*Paola picks another flower and slowly plucks the petals.*)
No, you cannot hear me... (*Approaching her*) But still, I must tell
you... Explain why you must leave... Why you cannot stay by my
side if ever you would be cured... For you I would always be "The
Jewess"... In my silence you would hear my lament, my condem-
nation... Your heart, your soul would never be at rest. They would
give you no peace... And again, you would be lost... Lost to me
once more... But this time, forever... (*Gesturing toward The Doctors*) So say these men, my child... Ah! How I love you!... But their
science says it, and it must be so! The decision is theirs... So be
it!... What does it matter how much more I must suffer? (*Raising her eyes heavenward*) Why?... Why?... What have I done?...
(*She stands for a moment in utter despair, then notices that Paola is
weeping.*) But... You are weeping...

175

Paola: Weeping?... Yes... (*Laughing*) Ha ha ha!... I was! I was!... Ha ha ha!... I am...

Géméa: Then our grief is eternal, and your God will be as silent as mine has been!

Paola (*staring into space*):   What? Can you not see Him?

Géméa: Give me the eyes of folly, and I shall!

Paola: Can you not hear Him?

Géméa: Give me the ears, ringing dizzy with madness, and I shall... Yes, I shall!... Oh, how I would blaspheme! But I shall not grieve your soul!... Yes, God of the Jew, God of the Christian...

Paola: He raises His blade above my head!

Géméa: God of the Jew, God of the Christian...

Paola: Be still! If you blaspheme, He will strike!

Géméa (*as if awestruck*):   Ah! Why do my words seem to freeze upon my lips?

Paola: You see? God is smiling... Your sacrifice is pleasing...

Géméa (*aside*):   Am I too going mad? What is this feeling...?

Paola (*suddenly, with a look of ecstasy*):   Oh! I remember... Yes!... I do! I do!... Like a cloud, lifting...

Géméa: Ah!... More, my child...

Paola: Growing clearer and clearer...

Géméa (*encouraging her*):   Yes!... More... Go on!

Paola: That day... Yes, I remember... That day... That day when I said no prayers... When my soul left my body...

Gémea: Go back!... Farther back... Far into the past... The past will give you back your reason... (*Pointing to The First Doctor*) He said so!... The man of science!... He knows...

Paola (*trying to recollect*): Ah... Clearer... Still clearer...

Gémea: Back... Farther... Farther...

Paola: Prayer... To fill my soul...

Gémea: The song they would sing to put you to sleep... *The Fishermen's Carol*... When you were a child... Remember?

Paola: Heaven's mercy... To fill my soul...

Gémea: And a woman was always there, by your side... Caring for you, watching you grow... Always there, like a mother... And oh, how she loved you!... Remember?... The pretty lady...

(*Bianca, helping Ottavio to his feet, stands with him, watching and listening.*)

Paola (*struggling to remember*): If only...

Gémea: Or is it Ottavio that you would remember?... Your Ottavio... Is it his memory that drives you on?... Would you see him?... (*Pointing*) There! Look!... Love him, my child! Love him as he loves you!... He is worthy of your love!

Paola: Oh, if only I... If only...

(*Just then, the organ of San Lucco can be heard, and a choir of women's voices begins singing the evening prayer. Paola stands listening, transfixed, surprised for a moment, and gradually growing more and more ecstatic.*)

Paola: Listen... The prayer!... The evening prayer!... (*Her face beams with a look of heavenly joy.*) Oh! I remember now!... I do! I do!... The prayer of my childhood...... The same... Yes, I remember!... How it frees my mind and refreshes my soul! (*She stands reciting a silent little prayer, then, falls to her knees.*) Almighty God!... Thou hast saved me with Thy mercy!

Bianca (approaching Géméa):   O fortunate mother! Embrace your child... A miracle has given her back to you!

Géméa (to Paola, placing her hand on her head, as if in benediction): Pray, my child... Pray...

Paola (hands joined):   O God! I have only my heart to know Thy ways... O Thou, who art naught but goodness and love... Those who love are Thy children... My mothers are Thy daughters... Sisters in devotion and sacrifice, O my God!... God of mercy and loving kindness, bless them... Oh, bless them...

Géméa: Pray, my child... Pray...

Paola: The hatred of centuries draws them apart. Burning passions sear their souls. But their hearts rise to Thee in a single act of love... Good mothers have they been, beyond all measure... Devoted, beyond all others... Let Thy hand reach out and bestow upon them Thy blessing... O my God, I pray you draw them together!

(*There is a long moment of silence.*)

Géméa (to Bianca, holding out her hand):   I forgive you, signora...

CURTAIN

Suggestions for Further Reading

Beaumarchais, Jean-Paul de, Daniel Couty, and Alain Rey. *Dictionnaire des littératures de langue française*. Rev. ed. Paris: Bordas, 1994.

Bell, Caryn Cossé. *Revolution, Romanticism, and the Afro-Creole Protest Tradition in Louisiana, 1718–1868*. Baton Rouge: Louisiana State University Press, 1997.

Blassingame, John. *Black New Orleans, 1860–1880*. Chicago: University of Chicago Press, 1973.

Brisbane, Era Mae. "Théâtre de Victor Séjour." M.A. thesis, Hunter College, 1942.

Les Cenelles: A Collection of Poems by Creole Writers of the Early Nineteenth Century. Translated by Régine Latortue and Gleason R. W. Adams. Boston: G. K. Hall, 1979.

Coleman, Edward Maceo. *Creole Voices: Poems in French by Free Men of Color First Published in 1845*. Washington, D.C.: Associated Publishers, 1945.

Cottin, John Richard. "Victor Séjour: Sa vie et son théâtre." Ph.D. diss., University of Montreal, 1957.

Coyne, Stirling. *The Woman in Red*. London, 1872.

Daley, T. A. "Victor Séjour." *Phylon* 4 (1943): 5–15.

Davidson, James Woods. *Living Writers of the South*. New York, 1869.

Desdunes, Rodolphe. *Nos Hommes et Notre Histoire*. Montreal: Arbor et Dupont, 1911.

Du Bois, W. E. B. *Black Reconstruction in America, 1860–1880*. Introduction by David Levering Lewis. 1935. New York: Atheneum, 1992.

Fabre, Michel. "New Orleans Creole Expatriates in France: Romance and Reality." In *Creole: The History and Legacy of Louisiana's Free People of Color*, ed. Sybil Kein. Baton Rouge: Louisiana State University Press. 2000.

————. "International Beacons of African-American Memory: Alexandre Dumas père, Henry O. Tanner, and Josephine Baker as Examples of Recognition." In *History and Memory in African-American Culture*, ed. Geneviève Fabre and Robert O'Meally. New York: Oxford University Press, 1994.

————. *From Harlem to Paris: American Writers in France, 1840–1980.* Urbana: University of Illinois Press, 1991.

Gates, Henry Louis, and Nellie McKay. *The Norton Anthology of African-American Literature.* New York: W. W. Norton, 1997.

Hatch, James and Ted Shine, eds. *Black Theatre USA: Plays by African Americans.* Vol. 1: *The Early Period: 1847–1938.* New York: Free Press, 1996.

Hemmings, F. W. J. *The Theatre Industry in Nineteenth-Century France.* Cambridge: Cambridge University Press, 1993.

Hoffmann, Léon-François. *Le nègre romantique: personnage littéraire et obsession collective.* Paris: Payot, 1973.

Kein, Sybil. *Creole: The History and Legacy of Louisiana's Free People of Color.* Baton Rouge: Louisiana State University Press. 2000.

Kertzer, David. *The Kidnapping of Edgardo Mortara.* New York: Knopf, 1997.

Korn, Bertram. *The American Reaction to the Mortara Case: 1858–1859.* Cincinnati: American Jewish Archives, 1957.

McCormick, John. *Popular Theatres of Nineteenth-Century France.* London: Routledge, 1993.

Moos, Herman. *Mortara: Or the Pope and His Inquisitors.* Cincinnati, 1860.

O'Connell, David. "Victor Séjour: Ecrivain Américain de Langue Française." *Revue de Louisiane* 1 (Winter 1972): 60–61.

O'Neill, Charles Edwards. *Séjour: Parisian Playwright from Louisiana.* Lafayette: Center for Louisiana Studies, University of Southwestern Louisiana, 1995.

————. "Theatrical Censorship in France, 1844–1875: The Experience of Victor Séjour." *Harvard Library Bulletin* 26 (1978): 417–41.

Perret, John. "Victor Séjour, Black French Playwright from Louisiana." *Teachers of French* 57 (Dec. 1983): 187–93.

Roussève, Charles Barthelemy. *The Negro in Louisiana: Aspects of His History and His Literature.* 1937. Reprint, New York: Johnson Reprint Corporation, 1970.

Savard, Félix. "M. Victor Séjour." *La chronique littéraire* 2 (June 1862): 48–55.

Séjour, Victor. *The Jew of Seville.* Trans. Norman Shapiro, with introduction by M. Lynn Weiss. Urbana: University of Illinois Press, 2002.

————. "The Mulatto." Trans. Andrea Lee. In *The Multilingual Anthology of American Literature,* ed. Marc Shell and Werner Sollors. New York: New York University Press, 2000.

———. *La Tireuse de cartes.* Paris: Michel Levy Frères, 1860.

Sollors, Werner. *Neither Black nor White yet Both: Thematic Explorations of Interracial Literature.* New York: Oxford University Press, 1997.

Tinker, Edward Laroque. *Les Ecrits de langue française en Louisiane au XlXe siècle.* Paris: Librarie Ancienne Honoré Champion, 1932.

———. *Les Cenelles: Afro-French Poetry in Louisiana.* New York: Spiral Press, 1930.

Viatte, Auguste. *Histoire littéraire de l'Amérique francaise des origines à 1950.* Paris: Presses universitaires de France, 1954.

Young Brisbane, Era. "An Examination of Selected Dramas of Victor Séjour including Works of Social Protest." Ph.D. diss., New York University, 1979.

Victor Séjour was born a free man of color in New Orleans in 1817. He left his native city at the age of nineteen for Paris, where he began a writing career. In 1837, Séjour published "The Mulatto," the first short story written by an African American. The Comédie Française performed *Diégarias* (*The Jew of Seville*), his first play, when Séjour was just twenty-six years old. Twenty of his twenty-two plays were performed in Paris and New Orleans between 1844 and 1875. Victor Séjour died in 1874 and is buried in Paris.

Norman R. Shapiro, professor of Romance languages and literatures at Wesleyan University, is a widely published translator of French poetry, prose, and theater. Among his works are *Four Farces of Georges Feydeau* (NBA nominee), *Fifty Fables of La Fontaine, The Fabulists French: Verse Fables of Nine Centuries* (ALTA Distinguished Book of the Year), *Selected Poems from "Les Fleurs du mal,"* and *One Hundred and One Poems of Paul Verlaine* (recent recipient of the MLA Scaglione Prize).

M. Lynn Weiss is an associate professor in American studies at the College of William and Mary. She is the author of *Gertrude Stein, Richard Wright: The Poetics and Politics of Modernism* (1998). Her more recent work is on Louisiana's Creoles of color.

SECOND LINE PRESS
LOUISIANA HERITAGE SERIES

second
line
press

New Orleans, LA

Composed in 10.5/13 Adobe Caslon
with Berkeley display
by Barbara Evans
at the University of Illinois Press
Reprinted with adjustments by Second Line Press